Kiss the Undertow

Kiss the Undertow

a novel

MARIE-HÉLÈNE LAROCHELLE

translated by
MICHELLE WINTERS

ARACHNIDE

Je suis le courant la vase © 2021, Leméac Éditeur (Montréal, Canada)
English translation copyright © 2024 Michelle Winters

First published as *Je suis le courant la vase* in 2021 by Leméac Éditeur
First published in English in 2024 by House of Anansi Press Inc.
houseofanansi.com

House of Anansi Press is committed to protecting our natural environment. This book is made of material from well-managed FSC®-certified forests, recycled materials, and other controlled sources.

House of Anansi Press is a Global Certified Accessible™ (GCA by Benetech) publisher. The ebook version of this book meets stringent accessibility standards and is available to readers with print disabilities.

28 27 26 25 24   1 2 3 4 5

Library and Archives Canada Cataloguing in Publication
Title: Kiss the undertow : a novel / Marie-Hélène Larochelle ; translated by Michelle Winters.
Other titles: Je suis le courant la vase. English
Names: Larochelle, Marie-Hélène, author. | Winters, Michelle, 1972- translator.
Description: Translation of: Je suis le courant la vase.
Identifiers: Canadiana (print) 20230581374 | Canadiana (ebook) 20230581382 |
ISBN 9781487012106 (softcover) | ISBN 9781487012113 (EPUB)
Subjects: LCGFT: Novels.
Classification: LCC PS8623.A7615 J4713 2024 | DDC C843/.6—dc23

Cover image: Montage by Julie Larocque, from an image by Stefano Zocca (unsplash.com)
Book design and typesetting: Lucia Kim

House of Anansi Press is grateful for the privilege to work on and create from the Traditional Territory of many Nations, including the Anishinabeg, the Wendat, and the Haudenosaunee, as well as the Treaty Lands of the Mississaugas of the Credit.

With the participation of the Government of Canada
Avec la participation du gouvernement du Canada | Canadä

We acknowledge for their financial support of our publishing program the Canada Council for the Arts, the Ontario Arts Council, and the Government of Canada.

Printed and bound in Canada

MIX
Paper from
responsible sources
FSC® C103567

Part One

∽ I ∾

DIAMONDS SHIMMER ON THE water's surface, the overflow sloshing into the drain just short of my feet. The liquid mass dances, distorting the markers at the bottom of the pool. The chips in the tiles open a trail in the weakened grout. My feet are the same sick yellow as the plastic, my wrinkled skin discoloured, my overgrown nails oxidized.

The drowning victims they fish out of rivers are swollen and blue, stretched over their swallowed fill. They are algae, mud, abyss. Slick and puffy, they become fish.

Nothing survives the dead water of the pool.

I snap the strap of my goggles and the rubber seals settle into the familiar creases. It feels like I'm wearing them when I'm not.

I slip on my short fins and dive.

My body tenses in the familiar cold. The moment I need the exertion, my system revolts, refusing to comply. Still, like the rest of us, I'll tell you I learned to swim before I could walk, using its seminal nature to convince myself I'm special. The ugly truth is we're a bunch of freaks stranded on the shore, rejected by the earth, struggling to compete in this unfriendly environment. It's a hell we adore.

The fins make my legs exhilaratingly pliant, streamlined. With my arms free from the need to propel, they perform exact, efficient pulls. I move with mechanical precision, hearing just my wet breath and the slapping of my feet. My goggles are fogged, distorting my view, though there's nothing to see. I orient myself instinctively, sensing my deviance from the course, predicting my distance from the wall, and the space I'll need to turn. My arms and legs pound the water in violent rhythm. I liquify.

⸺

Alexie grabs my shoulder. The sudden change of rhythm sends me headfirst into the wall. Crouching over the drain, she reaches a hand to help me out. I didn't hear him call an end to practice. The team sits in silence as he considers us, arms wrapped around his clipboard.

Alexie and I sit in back next to Mel and Seth, warmed by their shoulders' wet contact. Alexie slips her hand into mine and drapes herself against my shoulder. Her skin is dry, cracking at the joints, with thick wrists that don't show the bone like mine. She strokes my palm before sliding our fingers together.

He says nothing. With his foot, he slides up a cardboard box: the new suits for the Nationals. They're in individual bags, labelled with our names. The boys' packages are tiny—their suits are microscopic and they usually order just the one, where some girls have ordered five, as well as jammers. The box and the side of the pool empty bit by bit until it's just me and Lace, with her gymnast's body, all short, powerful muscles. I fake a few stretches, afraid I'm about to find out my cheque bounced and my order isn't there. There's a line of mildew running through the grout between the tiles. The gutters are full of it. I scrape some up with my nail. These little spores resist any disinfectant, multiplying day by day, gradually taking over, giving life to the concrete.

He's waiting for me to look him in the eye. At the mercy of his gaze, I give him my attention, and when he's sure he has it, he lets the moment drag. We're the same size, me and him. His yellow whistle hangs from a ribbon around his neck, with his initials written on it in permanent marker. He wears a faded blue T-shirt with the blue and gold Moncton colours, like we all do. His calves are shaved smooth like his forearms, even though he doesn't compete anymore. His face is blotched red against his blond hair.

He hands me the plastic pack with my three new suits.

—

I peel off my one-piece like a rind. The shower spits out an uneven stream, but at least it's hot. My muscles relax, my skin turns pink, my back unleashes a chlorinated steam. I chug the hot jet. The water forms a gutter down my neck and chest, disappearing into my pubic hair. Water shoots down my forehead, pools in my lashes, drips down the sides of my nostrils. I stick out my tongue and drink my shampoo runoff. A sludgy puddle forms around my feet.

I pull on my jeans without underwear, like we all do. The fabric catches my wet skin and I have to squirm my way into them. I drop my bathing suit and towel into my bag and leave the locker room without saying goodbye.

My stomach writhes, viciously hungry.

❧ 2 ❧

THE LIQUID TURNS green as I add the frozen kale. I wait for it to thicken up before adding the protein powder. It's revolting, but it'll fill me for a few hours. The smoke from the Vitamix engine stinks, but the familiar noise doesn't wake anyone. I slop my breakfast into my water bottle.

In the shared stairwell, someone has tracked mud up on their shoes. I zigzag around the prints on my way down. Kensington Market is already bustling. I nod to the fishmonger across the way under his busted blue-and-white awning before covering my head with my hood. The morning smells like beer and garbage. Everything is dirty, the sidewalks, streets, walls, people, just the way I like it.

We've been living in the Baldwin Street apartment for close to two years, so I guess I belong here. Lace, Alexie, and I were new to the team and none of us from Toronto, so we decided to look for a place together. Alexie wanted to live in Kensington, with the colours, shops and chaos, and Lace and I were looking for something close to the Athletic Centre.

Our landlord is a plaid-shirted old man who we haven't seen since we signed the lease. When we received his registered letter last year, telling us he'd raised the rent, we had to find a fourth roommate. The apartment only has three bedrooms; we had to split the living room. Vicki sleeps behind a velvet curtain.

I buy a mango on Spadina from a lady sitting on the sidewalk. Despite the weather, she's wearing tiny sandals with her heels hanging over the ends. Her toenails are encased in mounds of horned flesh. Her soles are blackened crusts, thick and hard like shoe leather. Her skin cracks open like worn cork. She looks at me through her empty, wrinkled lids.

The walk to the Athletic Centre warms me up, gradually loosening my leg muscles. At reception, Guido asks for my card, though he sees me every day. Hunched over his paunchy gut, it's hard to distinguish where he stops and his stool begins. He has a droopy mustache and big rosacea patches on his cheeks. He wrinkles his nose as I pass.

The locker-room floor has the same tiles as poolside, light-grey octagons separated by strips of dirty grout. The stagnant water creeps into the ceramic. The mop, pushed tirelessly by the round Puerto Rican staff, never seems to clean the chlorinated floor. I stop for a moment before the metal door that acts as a transfer chamber between the locker room and pool. A cold draft blasts from an unknown source, an icy gust constantly butting against the warm, wet air of the pool. My skin knows the contrast and reacts to the temperature clash before it happens. The shudder down my nape is no longer a shocked reaction, but a reflex. My body knows the routine: I grudgingly pull the door handle and the antiseptic air swooshes past, I crane my neck, rip out hair putting on my cap, rotate my shoulders and arms, stretch my calves, force my goggles into my eye sockets, flex, pose, dive.

You swim to the end of your breath, of your strength, then go farther; you delight in your pain, the water is your nemesis and ally. It's the fight itself. You become one with the element, melting together. No other discipline demands such absorption, such oneness, such penetration.

Over the years I've consumed gallons of pool water. It saturates my blood. In return, I leave my dead, toxic cells. I don't resist the poison anymore, I let it infiltrate me, coursing through my veins. Some master the waves, others the depths. For me, it's the poison. Breathing chlorine doesn't burn my lungs, swallowing it doesn't choke me, my skin takes on the synthetic blue. I disappear.

—

With the weight belt on, I overdo the pull-ups, sending flames down my back, arms, neck, and forearms. My shoulders may pop out of their sockets. Ten more. I focus on a point in the distance, ignoring the pain.

Sweat sticks my shirt's polyester to my back. Movements jerky, I drool on the bar. Eight more.

I close my eyes.

One last pull.

I drop unsteadily to the ground, finding my feet as the ceiling lurches overhead. People work out on machines all around me. I forgot they were there.

The sweat itches everywhere at once. I scratch the back of my neck, the itch moves down my back; I scratch my back, it moves to my inner thighs, my scalp, my calves. I step on the back of my sneakers and kick them off, pulling off my sweatpants; they're making me sweat. I'm wearing Alexie's shorts underneath. All of mine are dirty.

I gulp the rest of my water, plant my feet on the leg press, and release the weights. My thigh muscles

contract into a long diamond bulge I can't stop staring at. My body is a hybrid of manly curves, with the
thighs, shoulders, and trapezoids of a teenage boy. My
shorts yawn open when I flex.

The bench is nothing compared to the pull-up bar.
The reps are no problem, and I've just hit thirty when
Pete cuts in and straddles me, stretching out to kiss my
neck. I grit my teeth and thrust him onto the floor.
He laughs and goes to stand against a pillar with Seth.
I give them the finger.

The gym smells like Tiger Balm, which we smear on
like butter, tricking our aching muscles with camphor,
the athlete's heroin.

Alexie mops her face waiting for me, her loose hair
a mass around her head. My famished insides shriek.

I focus on the stream of water as I fill my bottle
from the fountain, but I can feel him behind me. His
stance, his weight … I didn't need to hear his footsteps;
his presence thickens the air. I take the time to drink
before turning to face him and am surprised to find
his arms uncrossed. Instead, he seems open. Pleased. I
read the card he hands me, digesting each word as he
explains. His voice is characteristically measured, but
I've come to know the enthusiasm in his gestures and
the squint of his eyes.

Among those of us picked to go to the Nationals,
he'll choose six to train this summer in Bordeaux,

France. Two weeks with the Girondins team. The knots in my neck and back slacken as he talks. He takes my face in his hands and tells me he wants me on the trip and that he believes in me. He slides the form wordlessly into my trembling hand.

The cold air outside the training room overpowers me. Suddenly dizzy, I lean against the wall and catch my breath. The cement is cool like the inside of a cave, and I poke my fingers into one of the conical holes of the panel. The edges are bumpy, with little rocks in the concrete. My back scrapes against them with each breath. I press my back hard into them, my hair snagging in the fissures. I stroke the reassuring roughness until the nausea passes. The wall's indentations mark my skin when I step away. I press my palm against the cement and watch the texture imprint itself.

∞ 3 ∞

THE COACH'S OFFICE is cramped and smothering.
I curl up like I'm home in bed. One glass wall looks
out to the pool, but a dusty film obscures the view. An
overused armchair sits in the corner, the fabric stained
from years of wet swimmers, a yellow patch marking
the centre. I sit on the patch, waiting.

A black filing cabinet leans against one wall, containing the club papers. The drawers don't close right and
creak on their tracks. Posters and announcements for
old events cover the stains on the walls, their corners
drooping.

He returns with the cameras. It's my job to install
them at either end of the lanes. I open the tripods,

attach and focus the lenses. The photos are taken on a timer. I empty the memory cards and go get ready.

I dive after Seth, using his wake to gain speed. His movements are slow, strong, and loose, spreading a tireless triangular wave out behind him. Vicky follows me, her fingertips grazing my toes when I slow down. Whirlpools form under my arms, the bubbles disappearing down my sides. A steady rhythm pounds between my thighs. My breath is oily, its greasy inhalations resisting the chlorine that invades my lungs with a stifled cough.

I smack my hand against the side and Seth comes up behind me, pressing himself against me through our thin layers of lycra. I pry myself out and go looking for my towel.

He'll be waiting at his place for me this afternoon. I try and catch his eye before I leave, but he's busy explaining something to Lace, holding a camera.

⁓

I enter the code on the keypad. The building isn't luxurious, but it's safe and well-maintained. He lives on the first floor and left the door unlocked.

The entranceway is narrow, with a patterned mat for his sneakers, shoes, and sandals. I recognize his coat hanging from a peg. He appears in shorts, bare-chested, and extends his hand to guide me to the back room. I walk through the tidy, sparsely furnished living room, where a bay window throws some of the sky's grey light. Dust particles float in the air.

He places the little powder envelope ceremonially in my palm. I should have held off another few days. He lays his hand on my forehead, sensing my need. His open palm soothes me, slowing my heart to normal. He traces a line with his finger down the centre of my face, over my lips and chin, shaking off my invisible filth. He closes his eyes and breathes.

Now we can start.

His hands crush my shoulders, flattening my bare feet against the floor. I'm not supposed to resist the weight, so I let the pressure bend me into a bow. He moves down my back until I'm on all fours. I take deep breaths, curving my spine. His hands are warm through my clothes, like his voice. He murmurs an old prayer, rolling his tongue. Lyle. I repeat it with him until my thoughts float away. My mouth is dry and I chew the word, sticking it to my palate. He does this with me, holding my head in his hands, moving it gently from side to side. The movement lulls me, making me feel less alone. I am the wave and the primal chant. The rhyming turns to a growl as he guides me but lets me vocalize. I clear my throat, unsticking an invisible film and sink deeper into myself. The rocking of my head increases, making me feel not so much dizzy as *cradled*. His rhythm has the ancient familiarity of generations I've never known, one loop leading to the next until I drift back to my own personal prehistory. I become fish, plankton, amoeba.

My hands leap from the ground in a flaming dance. The spark is born of water. He helps my body to evolve, guiding my ascension so I don't burn myself. I deliver myself to his instruction, to a destination only he knows. A trembling, or more of a vibration, starts up between my lungs, making me feel nauseous and a little drunk. I stretch out and the vertigo splits course, shooting up the back of my neck and down to my guts. The pleasure is depressing, like endlessly reliving a disappointment.

My eyes are open but unseeing, blinded by visions. The little wood-panelled room is meaningless, like the cushions spread out on the floor or the incense burning in the corner. Only he and I can open a new plane of unlimited dimension.

He presses into my hip bones, gouging my pelvis, balancing my ribcage like a husk he's about to crack. I ease into the agony, my bones snapping as if to break. But I behave. He chants a rasping hum as he quarters my limbs, and I join in the growling to overcome the pain. A primitive language escapes my throat, echoing his in a soothing, unexpected rattle. We've just begun to communicate in codeless tongues when he interrupts me with a hand. He alone has the right to sound, acting as our shared voice. I stifle my suffering and he shakes my shoulders until my head whips the air. In a dislocated frenzy, my reason dissolves.

When he releases me, I'm a formless mass. A sticky spill.

Somewhere, reality slams a door.

Time is hazy from the ground where I lie. My pores sweat, but my bones are frozen. No blanket or duvet can warm me back to life. My blood has stopped, my thoughts drained, but the loss is a comfort. Nothing is possible, nothing expected. A shiver finally sets in, returning me to life despite myself, and I reluctantly yield the abyss.

He slides an arm under my knees and one behind my neck, lifting me like a doll and setting me gently in bed. He continues the ritual with a few last strokes meant to sweep away my final impurities and lies down next to me, breathing peacefully into my neck. I expect nothing.

The sun is setting. Or is it coming up? I know this formless twilight; it's the state he creates for me, eradicating time and space in a world of water. A dry water, an impossible spirituality, mine to master. Soon, I find my feet and pull myself out of bed. I find my clothes and put on my shoes. He's still in there. I don't know if he's really asleep, but I cross the stark room and noise-lessly close the door. The air outside is too frigid for spring to break through. I want to go back inside. At the streetcar stop, everything returns to normal. I tap my card and sit on a worn seat, letting the creak of the rails rock me gently all the way home. I have no bag or baggage, a welcome state of undress, an artifice-free identity.

The effect of the powder has completely worn off, and I fight the coming-down migraine, more of a pressure than an ache, starting deep in my temples. The pain isn't as hard to handle as the feeling of empti-ness, of not knowing what's missing. I close my eyes lazily, still trembling, as much on my own as from the streetcar. I vibrate along with the other passengers, all together out of sync. When I open my eyes, I step off at my stop without a glance back.

4

IT'S BEEN WEEKS since I cut my nails and they're shredding, desiccated by the chlorine. I usually bite off the chips and chew the rinds, leaving my fingernails ragged and frilly, brittle. Today, I get out the clippers. The blades bend the wet tips before cutting them, a few of them peeling in layers. I'll need an emery board. My hands are pale and dry. I trace a big vein starting at my middle finger, following it down to my wrist like a blue worm beneath the transparent skin. I should be able to pierce the surface and let him out.

I don't need to check the clock; a red sun sprawls across the big bottom branch of the naked maple outside my bedroom window, so I know it's time. I dig in the basket for my track pants and two warm socks that I think are clean. My coat is buried in my sheets. I give a last check in my bag before closing it; my goggles are still drying in the bathroom. I close my bedroom door, holding the lock so it doesn't click. I push my finger into the rubber of the fridge door to break the suction, trying not to shake it. My shelf is almost empty. I put two yogurts in my coat pocket, then my goggles, and take a last look toward Vicki's velvet curtain. Her doorless room. Behind the heavy drape, I hear her soggy breath. She sleeps with her mouth open. I walk down our steps, put in my ear buds, and set out.

The light stays grey despite the sun, leaving no reflection in the dirty snow clinging to the sidewalk's lip, all the sparkle dead. The salt crunches under my soles. At least there's no ice. I put up my hood, then take it down when I see something on the ground. I speed up and cross the street to find a racoon, carcass intact, still new. It must have died on its way home, its nose and forepaws just touching the broken lattice of the neighbours' porch. The wood is chewed at the corner, which must be its entrance. Its tracks lead here in the thin snow; it was coming from the road and must have gotten hit.

The wind ruffles the dead fur on the scruff of the enormous raccoon. Before I moved to Toronto, I'd only ever seen one on a camping trip, and I remember it being smaller and sleeker. Here, they're round and massive, more imposing than cats. Its fur is complex; the roots are white, then darken, then turn white again, tipped with perfect black. I bury my fingers in the speckled density. I've never touched a raccoon. The body is cold, but the coat retains a fluffy warmth as I stroke furrows across its back, never to fill with life or breath. The long fur slides between my fingers, nestled against my hand. The firm body isn't stiff yet; I can still pinch a soft fold of skin. Accepting its playful invitation, I twist a strand around my index finger. I lean in closer from where I squat next to it until my nose is embedded in its pelt. The smell of its skin is subtle, like wood and mushrooms, dust and meat. It's clean. Bloodless. Its ears tuck into its neck, just soft little rounded triangles lined with velvety fuzz. I caress all of it, every part. My knees pop when I stand back up. I'm going to be late.

———

Practice goes long, the pool still full of the first swimmers who, at this hour, are mostly old people. Their curved backs, sunken chests, and droopy skin come to life in the water. Their bodies unfold, swelling with the suppleness of their bygone youth. Their strokes are slow but precise, their kicks regulated by a still-vibrant energy. On the steps, the women in their swim skirts wet their necks before jumping into the pool, their dabbing meant to absorb the shock of the cold. A few homeopathic drops to ease the harsh transition.

We, on the other hand, are trained for peak brutality, thinking one step ahead at all times; when you dive, you're already swimming; when you're swimming, you're already drying off. Moments blend with nothing in between, and order is essential, but also fluid. You have to be in the instant and the future at once. My mind can split time, out of pure habit. He's designed exercises for this purpose, like the Double Bind, executed while kneeling, folding your body twice. He makes us hold the pose over and over, forcing our chests to our thighs. Sometimes he'll lie down on top of us with all his weight. It kills your shoulders and hips, but they end up relaxing in a position where your joints dislocate. In an infinite S, we become Ouroboros, the snake eating its own tail, guardian of the cycles of time. Mastering the pose signifies an understanding of the perpetual, the departure also an arrival. All these exercises are supposed to improve our performance, simulating victory.

He didn't call me over this week. He has to work with another swimmer. We don't talk about this part of the training, but I know he sees others. I've seen the million little signs: a tampon in the bathroom waste basket, a long hair on the rug … He texts us. For his notifications, I chose a ringtone I'd never confuse with another one, but I sometimes hear it coming from other people's phones, and in a few quick seconds I'll go from giddy to devastated. There are weeks he doesn't invite me at all, and others where I'm there every day. During those times, I'll wake up in the middle of the night to see if he's messaged.

I try to read his face for signs of a potential invitation, but he's intent on his notes and doesn't look up. A little queue has formed around him for work after practice. When he leans forward to write, his hair falls over his eyes, and he does the thing where he tucks it behind his ear but it's too short and falls back down. The pointless gesture draws me in, makes me want to go over there. His hair at the roots is curly and thick, growing out into straight spikes. Like the rest of us, he's not really blond; it's bleached. All our hair is the same burned yellow, even the darkest of us.

I make my way to the locker room, resigned, not looking back, hiding my disappointment in my towel. I hold my chin high and strike a pose he doesn't see. I'll come back and swim later, once the longing has passed, when I can free myself from the deep knots in my stomach.

The shower stall is filthy. Hair clogs the drain and sticks to the plastic curtain. A soapy puddle forms around my feet and I pee carelessly into it. I didn't bring any soap and the dispenser is empty, as they often are. Some of us fill bottles with free soap to use at home, steal toilet paper … We cheat the pool wherever possible, feeling it somehow owes us. Whatever we take, that pool has robbed us of infinitely more. It's not a sacrifice, so much as an exchange that's almost friendly. Almost good-natured. I leave the shower feeling no cleaner, no dirtier, just with slightly less chlorine. I leave my hair wet and cover it with my hood. It'll dry in time.

I wear my flip-flops to class. The Science Building is just a few steps from the Athletic Centre. My usual seat is empty, so I sit, holding a place for Alexie. The auditorium slowly fills up, the desktops coloured by binders, sweaters, snacks. The air fills with the smell of sweet coffee. The coats on our seatbacks turn them into armchairs, and we lose ourselves in quilted down, imagining we're still at home, in bed.

I have a hard time staying focused. There are hundreds of us in this class, and all the little details catch my attention. The snow on the boots of the girl next to me has melted into a puddle that's creeping to the edge of the step leading down. If it keeps going, it'll wet the fur collar of the girl sitting in front of me. I watch the stream's progress as I take loose, scattered notes. Alexie's face rests on her fist, her skin folding with the pressure, her nose slightly mashed. She's melting too, the other half of her face hidden in her thick pile of hair.

The heat soon becomes unbearable, and I'm glad I'm wearing flip-flops. The sweat on my neck itches and I scratch it with my pen. Alexie pulls her hair up in a ponytail. The girl with the wet boots takes off her sweatshirt, the advancing pool stopping just short of the fur hood below.

I'm hungry. A cramp slowly digs its way through my stomach, so I direct my attention to the faceless prof, who's so far away he could be man or woman. I take out a can of coconut water. It's warm, but the sugar fills me. We're always hungry. It's worse for the boys; some of them wake up in the middle of the night to eat. I do too. I'll get up and have a bowl of cereal or cold meat if there are leftovers. I dream of food.

With my chin in my palm, I scribble up the page. My wrist has a chlorine smell no shower can wash away. I poke out the tip of my tongue and lick my bleached skin. It has no taste, flaking in the dry, white folds. I cross my legs. The seam of my jeans slices into my crotch. You get used to it when you don't wear underwear. I writhe in my seat and the seam cuts deeper. I do it a few more times.

There are twelve minutes left in class, despite whatever the clock on the wall says. Those hands just spin aimlessly. No one uses it. In the pool, there are four wall clocks: two with regular numbers and two with multiple hands so you can start your timer no matter when. I can subtract my time to the millisecond without even thinking. I only need to glance at the start and finish clocks to gauge my performance. In competition you don't need this skill since your time is posted right in front of your lane. In some pools, the sensor you hit at the end of the lane is also a timer, but I don't have to check to know my time. Those numbers dance around me everywhere I look. I recite them, rank them, recognize them all around me: on billboards, menus, price tags. When I swim, I can count the seconds by calling out my movements. I'm conditioned to count time as I go, especially when I'm walking.

A wave of movement lets me know class is over, and the hundreds of us pack up our things. My open page is scrawled with random notes. I stuff everything in my backpack and hurry to catch up with Alexie, already out of her seat. We're going to Bloor for bao and bubble tea.

We still have to stop by the locker room for our coats and boots, and to dump our textbooks. We throw everything in our lockers, starving. The few minutes keeping us from food are unbearable, making the snow look like mouth-watering sugar cones. It's warmed up suddenly and the snow has turned to big crystals, melting in streams. Tomorrow will be summer.

We walk up Spadina to Bloor, arm in arm. Alexie is

supple like a vine, walking with her shoulders, so the top of her body seems to propel her instead of her legs. I stagger behind, holding on.

The frail body of the Vietnamese woman at the counter at Banh Mi Boys makes me think of Vicki's; the way she moves, the way she holds herself when she knows he's looking at her, with her scrawny legs. I order a single vegetarian steamed bao. Alexie cocks her head and huffs. I've let her down. She ordered three.

The steamed bun melts between my molars, the sticky skin of the mushrooms sliding down my tongue. It's delicious. I have sauce in the corner of my lips, saliva flooding my mouth. I get back in line to order two more. Alexie teases me, giving me a thumbs up for my failed restraint. We eat with our fingers, devouring little sandwiches from an Asia we don't know. The sauce drips down our palms and we lick them, laughing greasily. Soon, our trays are empty and we're still famished. We'll permit ourselves a bubble tea.

We take Bloor back to Bathurst to get to Kung Fu Tea. Alexie wants to do some shopping first. I watch as she tries on flowered tops that all look the same to me, trying to imagine how she'd like me to react. She leaves the shop happily, paper bag in hand. I smile too, for the tea I'll soon have earned.

The bubbles of tapioca sink to the sweet bottom of my drink. I stab a big bubble with my straw and suck it up greedily. The tapioca bursts between my ecstatic teeth. Alexie fishes the sticky black bubbles from hers as they climb up through the straw to her brown, sugar-frosted lips. She talks while she drinks. We make fun of the other customers, mostly Korean girls, giggling behind their hands. Eventually they get up and stomp out, their short kilts shimmying. I laugh so hard I spit a tapioca ball on the table. We hang out a while longer before finally agreeing to leave. Behind us, a Korean woman cleans up our mess, pushing the chairs back into the table.

5

EVERY BREATH LIGHTS a fire in the base of my throat, searing right through to my ears as I do a flawless crawl, my stomach knotted in one big cramp. The strain of kicking makes me lose control of my bladder and I pee without losing speed, my pelvis twisting with the rhythm of my alternating strokes. I stay on course. A wave forms around my body, cloaking my movements, and I force myself past, swallowing it.

I flip-turn too deep and lose time coming back up. I take up the final sprint furiously, a violent juddering in my guts. I slap the edge and pull myself up to puke in the drain. Thick bile hangs from my lips and I can't catch my breath. My mouth fills with a sour saliva I can't seem to spit out. A second surge of nausea wells up and I'm too spent to cough out the stream coming out my nose and mouth. I rest my cheek against the edge, bobbing in my own phlegm.

My legs are overwhelmed with an itch, but I don't have the strength to scratch it. I hang off the side, spluttering in the others' waves as they finish. I rest on my elbows just above the surface and let my body slap against the edge.

When I feel strong enough, I climb out, legs trembling. I steady myself with one hand against the wall, which is tiled in the same pattern as the floor, so I can't tell which is which. Up is down and I float in a shapeless space between the two. I can feel him watching me. His whistle screams, reverberating in my throat. Lyle. I swallow it up and poke my nails into the wall grout, tacky with humidity, returning me to earth. Alexie slides a reassuring arm around my shoulders and I blow my nose in my towel. The last group has just finished up and crawls out of the pool. Practice has wrecked us.

His face is blank, his eyes veiled in a cool, blue indifference. They're actually turquoise, unless it's just the water's reflection. Sometimes when I look at him, I think they have no colour at all and just absorb the hues nearby. I'm invisible to him right now, a formless part of the team. He's satisfied with us. I could be anyone.

As I listen, I chew on a corner of my towel, fraying

a loose seam. It has the same mildewy smell as all my clothes. Everything stays wet too long. My canine punctures the terrycloth and I don't bother even looking. I'm busy studying Pete's back, his pale white skin pocked with acne and red blotches. His shoulders are enormous compared with his waist. He's like an outboard motor, his whole body like an engine. His dick is like the rest of him, short and thick. I rest my chin in the crook of his neck, against his warm, comforting sweat. He leans his head back against mine and my hair falls over his shoulder.

He finishes up his notes and lets us leave. He didn't look at me.

Disappointment cuts a trench in my stomach, dragging down the corners of my mouth, hunching my shoulders, hollowing my chest. My whole body sulks. I lumber away from the Athletic Centre. The faces of strangers on the street blend together into him. He's everywhere. I want to scrape the bark off the trees, crunch my teeth into the sidewalk to stifle the need. Stuff my mouth with cotton, stitch up my eyelids.

———

The nights are never black in Toronto, but a grey diffused by billboards and streetlights. I wanted to walk home alone. The stink of the street, human and animal, doesn't scare me. I understand the moans of despair of these men and women, stained by the night. I just haven't lived it. The nighttime sadness smells of urine and vomit. I pass through it like a curtain.

It's warmed up already, melting the snow, leaving only piles of dusty sand.

My insides are heavy and my mouth is dry from the beer, pasting my tongue to my palate. I'm suddenly nauseous and cough up a wave of hot, thick spit. I punctuate my stagger with loogies. Almost home.

I pass a gang of stupid, skinny girls all wearing the same tight dress and too-high heels, clicking in step with each other. I pull my hoodie down over my eyes. I'm just a set of shoulders. In the dark, I pass for male.

At the corner of Nassau, a body lies wrapped in a filthy sleeping bag beneath an overturned baby carriage. It's barricaded by piles of garbage and smells like death.

At Baldwin, I stumble on the sidewalk, smashing my knee on the concrete. Through the hair covering my eyes, I can make out two forms, one round and one triangular. Both perfectly still. I struggle upright and lean back on my wobbly arms. Right next to the body of the dead raccoon is a vulture. I blink, and blink again. He's still there. His shoulders are massive, the twin bumps of his wings jutting upward, his skinny neck lost in the flange of his shoulders. I can't see his beak or eyes, but he bows down and shows me the top of his bald head, claws curled on the pavement. Magnificently ugly. He watches as I pass.

I throw up again before I reach the apartment, leaving a lumpy puddle in the stairwell before closing the door behind me.

The few metres to my bedroom look like miles, and I collapse in the living-room armchair. I burrow my head into the cushions while my feet seem to float, sending me into a queasy reverie of recycled horrors. Behind my eyelids, fractal figures dance. I'm going to puke again. An acidic foam rises to my lips, and I sleep at last.

∾ 6 ∾

WE CRAM TOGETHER in an empty subway car, sitting three to a seat despite all the room. Our cackling deters anyone thinking of getting on. The passengers on the platform wrinkle their noses and turn away. Alexie is spinning like a stripper around one of the poles and we egg her on, then Pete gets up and does some drag with her that's actually quite good. Someone puts music on their phone and cranks the volume. Here we go. The bar of the window frame pushes into my back as I sit crushed under the weight of Mel, who sits between my legs. The subway smells like dust and chewing gum. And pee. We don't notice the stations skimming by; we've got a whole Friday night to go with no morning practice.

A woman finally ventures into our car and sits as far from us as she can. Enormous Seth gets up and takes the seat next to her, fuelled by our catcalls. He tries to talk to her, flirting sarcastically. She holds her purse to her chest and tightens her lips, ignoring him. We tell Seth he's an idiot and she's not interested, but he goes at it harder, getting down on his knees. She won't look at him, instead trying to catch the eye of one of us girls, but we just laugh at her. She gets off at the next station, escaping Seth's cruel proposal. Our train leaves her there at Davisville station, and we wave as she disappears on the concrete horizon.

At Lawrence station, we jostle out onto the platform, dizzy from the trip. I hang from Alexie's arm. Mel bumps his hip in the tiled staircase, trying to race the people on the escalator, and makes a big show like he's injured. When we're finally outside, it's warm as summer. Toronto has no seasonal transitions. We buy beers on Yonge street and drink them as we walk, arms around each other.

We look lost, but we know where we're going.

The neighbourhood is quiet in the early evening. The sidewalk is too narrow to hold us all, and we spill out onto the road, infesting the realm of the rich.

That's the plan.

At the corner of Mount Pleasant, the boys decide to piss in someone's hedge. They'd love to get caught, but there's no one around. Nighttime makes us invisible. A warm breeze blows Alexie's hair. I close my eyes and follow the broad shoulders of my friends. Mel wants to stop at the Toronto French School, but there's nothing to do there; their pool is indoors. The 124 comes by and we hesitate, not knowing which way it goes on Bayview, so we take the avenue north on foot.

Post Road is paved—rich people don't drive their cars on just anything; the whole avenue is interlocked. Toronto's most expensive mansions hide up here behind ancient trees. They're palaces dwarfed by massive lots, a cold luxury where the only watchful eye is the alarm system. Security sees all. We walk in silence, a sign of respect we'll soon shake off. For now, we're hunting. In the distance, a Filipino woman walks a dog on a leash. A member of the staff. I crouch in a shrubbery and watch as the others flatten out under some pine branches. Seth climbs an oak, nimble as a cat. I dig my fingers into thick wet moss like pubic hair and tear out a tuft, burying my nose in it and licking the curly ends. The woman passes by without seeing us. She's wearing ear buds and speaking into the microphone, lost in conversation as she arrives home. When she laughs, we hear the lapping of the Indian Ocean. We mean her no harm; she's our mother, our sister.

We spy the bunker, a polished stone fortress protected by a wrought iron gate. The driveway is clear and the curtainless windows reveal an empty house. It's almost too easy. Mel and Pete are already climbing the fence. I stand against a tree trunk and wait.

At the boys' signal, we regroup. It wasn't as secure as it looked. The ground smells like wet grass and mushrooms and my feet sink in like a carpet. I hold in a burst of laughter and follow the others, already headed behind the house. When we reach the backyard, an automatic light turns on. I freeze, ready to run, but nothing happens. Before us stretches the magnificent shaded pool, bordered on one side by a natural stone wall creeping with young ivy. On the other side, a stand of dried bamboo separates the pool from the tennis courts. The retaining walls are all made of frosted concrete and marble. There are enough loungers for all of us.

I close my eyes. The cushions have been put away and the seats aren't very comfortable, but it doesn't matter. I run my finger along the blond wood, picking the thick coat of varnish with my nail. I wonder if the lives of these people are as smooth and shiny as everything they own. Their days must sparkle. I throw myself straight from the chair into the pool, the water salty and warm as a bath, like gelatin. My wake leaves a slimy outline you can almost see. The dim light from the balcony casts long shadows, and I run my hand over the water's surface, tracing circles, hypnotized by its dense warmth. Our trespasses create waves the drain can't hold.

We dive all together and scream out our triumph underwater. This house belongs to us. We're the first swimmers this pool has known and for close to an hour, we froth it up like cream, then collapse in a heap. No one thinks to get dressed.

Overhead, the canopy of branches shields us from the night. My head rests on Lace's stomach and I breathe in her salty skin. She's already tanned from the summer, browned golden like a croissant. I bury my nose in her belly button, tickling her like a child. When she gets up to escape me, Seth pushes her in the pool, unleashing another mass dive. Someone holds my head underwater with my face crushed into someone else's crotch. I grab at it and squeeze so I can get up and catch my breath. When I spit in Mel's face, he mashes his lips against mine and swims away.

I don't see the flashlight beam right away, but the scrambling of the others catches me up. It's the thrill we started to worry we might not get. At last, we're free to howl like the animals we are. I'm a piglet, a wild boar. I claw the earth, turning up dirt clumps as I stampede to the cobblestones of salvation. Only at top speed can I reassume human form, clutching a handful of clothing I grabbed on the way. The shouts of the security guard double my pace. The night scalds my throat and I cough out blackness and salt, losing steam.

By the time we catapult out onto Bayview Ave, naked and wheezing with laughter, no one is chasing us. We throw ourselves into a bush and get dressed. We didn't grab enough T-shirts, so the girls take them. Pete ends up in just his underwear, thrilled at the chance to parade himself before the indifferent subway. We laugh the whole way to Spadina, eager for the joy of exhausted sleep. I convulse with hunger alone in my seat. I could buy a hot dog when we get there, but I don't have any money. Alexie might have some, but I should just wait until I get home. My hair is still in wet tangles, dampening my borrowed T-shirt. I shiver again. Lace passes me her cigarette, which warms me up, calming my stomach and head in a little internal whirlwind that passes, leaving only soothing smoke. The warm air has cooled.

We transfer at Trinity Bellwoods, but the streetcar doesn't come. Stranded on the sidewalk, we scream, outraged at every passing car. My head is pressed between the concrete embankment and Mel's bare legs, his stubble scratching my face. I'm tracing the cracks in the pavement with my finger when a flash of light passes, spraying dust in my eyes. I have to pee. With the streetcar nowhere in sight, I struggle out from under Mel and slip into the park.

Still facing Dundas, I stop behind the first tree and

watch between my feet as the stream creeps past my sandals. Pulling up my shorts without standing, I notice a familiar shape to my left. We're the same height with me crouching and him standing, skinny and hairy on his skeletal legs. The vulture. His feathers are dull in the park's shadow, and he looks like he's broken. Two deep nostrils pierce the sides of the crooked beak he turns to look at me, imposing himself with a step in my direction.

He's hurt. I can sense it from him, though I see no wound. It's the suffering in his eyes. I reach for his bald skull, the skin softly wrinkled. I sink my fingers into the thin, naked folds, creating waves of flesh, losing myself in the rough caress.

In the distance, the streetcar squeals on its tracks, taking off without me.

I'm alone in the park, squatting in the hot puddle of my own piss.

⚭ 7 ⚭

THE WHISTLE HAS no tone. It's a scream, a cry, an animal release. My head beats in time with his forced rhythm, my hair in my eyes. I lose control, surrendering myself in an act of pure liberation. My body moves without me. A groan works its way up from deep inside and I release it at last, a lament without sadness, a death rattle from the diaphragm. He pushes on my abdomen, clutching the back of my head. My cry turns to a bleat as I dizzily swing. My pelvis grinds into the thin cushion and I'm distracted by the hardness of the wood when I'm supposed to be fully engaged in the thumping. Repeating the mantra builds a controlled violence, and I give in to the repetition, to the swinging, the tossing, the smacking, the flailing.

He pushes his finger into my mouth, crushing the powder inside my cheek. The mucous gets thicker and I feel the wave crash down the back of my head, into the roots of my hair, before the welcome warmth slides down my spine. I'm suspended, unable to feel his hands, but I know they're there. He hasn't abandoned me. I feel him everywhere, filling my pores. The ground loses its hardness, and I'm set to ascend. I wait. My fingertips are numb, so I chant louder. I could open my eyes if I wanted, but I don't have the strength. I float.

He suddenly grabs me under my shoulders and folds me forward before flipping my torso violently back. My head flops along. He does this a few more times before dropping me, limbs sprawled obliquely. He takes hold of my feet and flips me over on my front so I'm stretched out like a starfish, my nose bent against the cushion foam, blocking my breath. He smacks his palms against the soles of my feet, my calves, thighs, buttocks, up to my shoulders. It burns, but I don't make a peep. He applies pressure to each of my joints. I'm beaten, defenseless.

—

Between the curtain panels, I can see the next swimmers warming up. The girls are on the semi-final fifty-metre backstroke, then the boys do the hundred-metre butterfly, then my group, the fifty-metre crawl. The team files past. Elimination takes only a few minutes. The boys loosen their shoulders, crack their necks, pound their quads to stimulate response. It's a little superstitious, but they're deadly serious. From this point on, they won't look at or speak to anyone.

The Athletic Centre bleachers are packed. We're hosting, so we've got home advantage, swimming in our own pool with no jet lag. A class of rowdy kids sits above us, all with their phones out. The balconies are draped with the banners of every Canadian team, grazing the hands of the first-level crowd, lying on the railings like they're not supposed to. On one bench, I recognize the basketball team. I wave to Alexie's mom, who's brought her two little brothers. The robotic voice of the announcer overtakes the buzz of the crowd. The events are so short that he only has time to announce the lane, swimmer, and university before announcing the finish times. Poolside, the coaches and teams shout encouragement in the same rhythmic chant as the swimmers' breath. Their echoes collide.

I help Alexie into her suit, holding the strap so she can wriggle her arm into the narrow casing. The new girls' jammers are so tight we can't put them on alone, but the compression bumps you a good tenth of a second. Alexie helps me into mine. I slide my hand through the tiny hole and contort myself into the strap, then I slip off my bikini top through the neck. My breath shortens, and I mutate, pulling on my cap and goggles. The roar goes silent. Packed into my gear, I transform. My body loses contour and I'm a machine, a torpedo, a rocket.

The boys' competition is in high gear. We step out from behind the partition and warm up. They've given me lane five, where a guy from UBC is currently powering along. I'm already in there with him. I loosen my shoulders, do a few leg pumps and neck rotations. I'm alone, the UBC swimmer gone. My internal whistle sounds.

The judges enter the scores on the boards. My group gets into our spots, systems synchronized. The surface of the water resumes perfect stillness. I push my goggles into my eye sockets and crouch in position as my muscle fibres tense, expanding the lycra.

The whistle is a whip. I throw myself forward as far as I can and a few underwater strokes win me precious inches. When I come up for air, I've covered half the lane. I kick with all my strength, my arms and legs smacking the weightless surface. I'm in and out of the water at once, blind, only sensing the edge approaching, diving to make a tight turn that braces me forcefully against the side. I coil like a spring and turn with an explosive push. I surface instantly, already preparing to finish. I swim violently, my arms and legs like the blades of an eggbeater, frothing the pool. My shoulders lift with the force that holds me at the water's surface. My hand cracks

44

against the side and I feel my wrist crunch the whole way up my arm. We all touch at the same time. I check my score; I'm second, beating my own record. I climb out, my muscles still burning with tension. I scrub at my strained flesh. It feels like it might burst.

I snap off my bathing cap and squirm out of the unbearable jammer, the straps digging into my armpits, cutting my chest. Sweat rolls down my back, mixing with my wet hair. I could drink the whole pool, I'm so thirsty. I hold myself back, taking just take a few gulps.

They slap me on the back and congratulate me while he grips my neck and bestows his solemn praise.

Alexie didn't make it to the finals for this round, so I contain my joy. Only Vicki did, and she finished third, earning just a glance from him.

I still have the hundred-metre butterfly and two-hundred-metre freestyle to go, but there's a good half-hour before that. I pull on my hoodie so my muscles don't seize and look for my Thermos in the team's clutter. They built folding bleachers for us, but we messed them up instantly. It's hard to even find a spot to sit down. There are more bags than swimmers, and I dig through the chaos until I find mine.

Before I left this morning, I made a smoothie with what was left on my shelf in the fridge. It's disgusting, but I'm starving and need the liquid energy.

Alexie congratulates me from inside her towel.

She's clearly disappointed, so I just give a little smile. We watch the boys rush past in their butterfly laps. It doesn't matter what we do, their events will always be more exciting. You can feel it in the crowds; they're twice as loud for the men. The pools churn with their waves. Swimming itself isn't much of a spectator sport, but the boys manage to bring it home in a way we can't. It's tough for female swimmers to land a sponsor.

Lace comes up and kisses me on both cheeks. She was eliminated in the semi-finals. Today, she's just here for support. She probably didn't even wear her bathing suit under her track pants. I wanted to wake her up before I left, but she wasn't there. She won't tell me where she was.

Smile noted, she turns her attention to the pool. I wonder who she spent the night with. She racks up conquests, but never brings them home. We all agreed on that. It's distracting in the midst of practice and classes, and we can't be getting woken up at all hours by comings and goings. The place isn't even big enough for the four of us. I follow Lace's eyes to try and see which team her *friend* is on. She's hard to read, standing there silently, locked up tight, but somehow joyful too. I watch the results light up the board. Seth, Pete, and Mel qualified.

I peek at the timer on the wall and permit myself another gulp of my smoothie.

The next girls put in the starting block grips for the

back crawl. I'm not in this one, because I'm no good at it. Another peek at the timer and I have to get ready. I ball up my hoodie and stuff it in my bag with my water bottle. A hand grips my shoulder as I approach the warmup curtain.

Still holding on, he pulls me away behind an equipment box. I have to nail this one. Breaststroke is my event and I should feel it in my guts. He places his hand on my abdomen, his spread fingers covering me. I swallow and look around. His hand is still there. His eyes burn into my soul for another moment, then he turns and steps away, his attention elsewhere.

My chest is still crushed in my suit. I look at my feet. My toes are so pale they're transparent, my skin shriveled and wet. I should have cut my toenails. On my way to the staging area, one of our team yells something I can't make out.

A girl I don't know helps me into my suit. I stand perfectly still, letting my eyelids drop, retreating into myself. I take a huge breath and puff out my torso. My shoulders broaden, my throat opens, my chest expands. My stomach is flat, dense, and hard.

I'm on the starting block. At the far end of the lane is a poster I set as a goal to reach as fast as humanly possible. Two laps there and back. I am the ultimate machine, oiled to perfection, the seconds ticking down through my greased wheels. I slide through time. It's mine.

Part Two

Part Two

∾ I ∾

I SWITCH THE basket to my other shoulder to get down the narrow staircase. The laundry room is in the basement of the building, in a dark alcove that smells like mildew and booze. It's also where the recycling goes. A mountain of beer bottles sits waiting for some tenant to finally get up the courage to deal with them. A sticky pool spreads out from beneath it, the squalid mass looking like it might get up and walk on its own.

Four washing machines and two dryers stand in the far corner surrounded by dust bunnies and fluffs of thread like filthy little nests. I stuff an armful of clothes into one of the machines and dump some soap in the crusted hopper. The machine vibrates and rumbles as it chews my laundry. The cycle takes close to an hour.

I pull the chain on the naked bulb and step outside, straight across the street to the racoon.

The carcass has shrunk, like it's deflated. There are pits in the fur filled with scabby wounds. It's being eaten from the inside, the busy maggots moving in waves under the skin. The warm breeze ruffles the pelt, now a patchy velveteen. The snout is intact, the nose like a shiny rubber button. I stroke the bridge of the nose upward toward the eyes, now dried sockets. It's still soft and warm, resisting decomposition. The stiffness of the body doesn't affect the tail, which I can still wrap around my fingers. It's threadbare but glorious. Beneath the long hairs, the bone is finely pointed. There's a break at the end from an ancient fracture. I manipulate the deformity, groping for the story, the adventure. Clumps of fur stick to my fingers, revealing the bare bone in spots. I broke it.

I wipe the strands on my sweatshirt and pull up my hood.

The sky is heavy with a humidity that won't break. The cotton of my top sticks to my back. I hesitate for a second then head for Kensington Market.

The stores' wares are laid out on the street for pedestrians to weave through. The awnings are hung with army surplus pants, caps, and bags that skim your head as you pass, getting dirtier every day as they await their elusive buyer. Candy stores are nestled in next to cosmetic stores, butchers, thrift shops, florists, dispensaries. Tourists can't get enough of the reeking disarray, wading through the vapor that binds them in an improbable unity. I'm the child of the impatient mother, of the father smoking in his ratty Panama hat, of the woman clutching her purse, or the one whose plastic heels click on the greasy tar, of the bare-chested teenaged boy, of the Black guy in his house slippers. I rub against the crowd, merging with their oily mass until I come away wearing it.

—

His apartment sits at the top of a hill lined with drooping willows that block my way. My sandals beat a rhythm that I hum along to like an aggressive nursery rhyme. Lyle. My teeth whistle against the consonant, the flow of the old melody transporting me. My throat is a cavern of nerves and hope, my giddy footfalls spinning my mind. For all the sweet anticipation, I speed up, a maze of shortcuts unfolding ahead as I move forward going backwards, the summer tar sticking to my soles.

As I reach the doorstep, the taut string of my need turns into a migraine at the base of my skull.

He greets me in silence, leading me by the hand to the bedroom. I forget about shape and surrender to depth.

Despite the heat, there's an underground chill in the room where he sits me on a straw mat I've never seen. He slips me out of my clothes with a murmur to tell me we're starting. I close my eyes and open my mouth to receive the powder, climbing in to join him in his endless silence.

It starts off gently, with his fingers stroking my body, warming my skin in circles. The ensuing attack doesn't surprise me and in fact is a relief, matching the fog brought on by the powder. I'm shaken aimlessly, pulled by my feet, carried, my legs stretched wide to the breaking point. My back scrapes against the rough mat. My tendons snap, my pelvis spreads in a medieval torture. He tenderizes my bones like meat, digging his fingers into the pockets of my flesh, emptying them out. My cartilage softens. I liquify.

The blows bounce off me without impact. I absorb them, having long since accepted them as part of me. I respond to his inward pressure by pushing out, evacuating tension. He manipulates my spine, each vertebra bursting beneath the force of his fists. The release is over too soon, and I dangle, taut.

The stench of burned grease hangs thickly on me, a human sharpness, followed by a surgical stink. He's incinerated part of me.

He stuffs a felt tip in my mouth that leaves fuzz on my tongue, anaesthetizing my gums and cheeks.

I don't feel his bites. He devours my nose and chews my cheeks as a gooey mucus stretches between us. I'm sticky with him. His thumbs lick my forehead, smoothing the upset skin like a fold of pastry.

I am a carcass scoured of organs, ribs exposed, blood drained. I've offered myself on the altar, and now I lie empty, still.

∞ 2 ∞

I FORGOT MY clothes in the machine and they sat there all night, mildewing. The smell of fungus is embedded deep in the fibres and will take some work to get out. I dump a load of bleach into the reservoir and boil my clothes, my back bumping against the shaking drum. This time I'll wait it out. The raw concrete is clammy against my thighs, and I scratch out hunks of its powdery sediment.

A girl from the building comes stomping down the stairs and plants herself in front of me, wicker basket in her hands. She's clearly put out that I'm using the machine, though there are three others. Her basket holds a few slinky items that look already clean. Her arms are skinny, her pout greasy with lipgloss. Her hair is in a carefree chignon worn low. I loll back against the machine and close my eyes as she fills the machine next to me, muttering. I hear her hesitate at the door, turning back to consider her precious wash, then gathering up her expensive soap and basket, mumbling to herself up the stairs.

The garbage pile has grown, with some busted furniture thrown in the mix: a gutted chair, what must have been a bookshelf, a set of bedposts … I have a look through. Lying amid the detritus is an abandoned coat rack. When I pick it up, I disturb a big rat busily chewing a condom from a garbage bag. He doesn't look up. I leave him to it and pull out the grimy coat rack. It's in good shape, solid. A hanger still dangles from one of its arms, the bar covered in a worn velour, matted with dust and bare in spots. I bring it over next to me at the machine and the hanger sways over my head.

The base is massive, made of a black wood, balanced out at the top by horn-like metal hooks. The stand is just a column of the same dark wood as the base. The whole thing is peeling varnish in big strips, releasing a smell of rancid wax that leaves a coating in my throat. A big stain covers much of the base.

I stuff my wash into the dryer and wrestle the coat rack up the stairs. It's heavier than I'd thought and hard to get around the corners of the staircase. When I get to my room, I reek of sweat.

It dominates the cramped space, everything else seeming to revolve around it. I admire it from where I lie on my bed, and a warm breeze from the window rocks the hanger.

I slide a hand down my shorts, finding the familiar wetness. I stroke myself to the rhythm of the wind, slowly digging deeper. The air directs me, and I obey. From my damp flesh, a warmth takes root, creeping all the way up to the base of my skull. A moan escapes my lips as I grunt rhythmically, saliva bubbling in my mouth. I swallow the foam. Behind my eyes, there is only emptiness. The unfathomable void. My fingertips probe the holes, explore the peaks and detours until they find the right vibration, opening my stomach and hollowing me out with a bitter orgasm.

The hanger has stopped.

∾ 3 ∾

CRUSHED AGAINST THE car window, I swim in the wind, playing with a ball of air I hold in my hand. Four of us are crammed in the back seat, with Mel in the hatchback. I open my mouth and the gusts fills my cheeks as I swallow giant gulps. Seth sticks his head out the passenger side window and spits on a swaying transport truck. Howling like a wolf with his tongue lolling, he terrifies a family in a minivan. We laugh our heads off. Alexie passes me a beer, and Lace puffs big clouds of smoke with her cigarette that we try to grab before they dissolve. I take a sip of warm beer, trying to calm my nausea.

Pete's driving in his bathing suit, an open beer can between his legs. We know we're almost there when we see the signs for Sandbanks. The sky is white on the horizon, heavy with rainy-day warmth.

There's no lineup at the gate since it's still too early for tourists. We park carelessly and tumble from the car, leaving it unlocked. Seth climbs out through the window. We forget about Mel in back and he has to crawl over the seats. As we invade the beach in a clatter of cans, a few families move their towels farther down. Someone grabs me around the waist and I'm suddenly submerged, fully clothed. Seth climbs on my shoulders and I sink, choking on his tongue in my mouth. I bite his lip and escape, but he's already off, jumping on Vicki.

My T-shirt floats out from my body like a jellyfish. The flat, grey lake holds me gently at its surface, and I close my eyes under a fine drizzle, washing the sand from my face. The drops pool in my eyebrows, slide into the hollows of my eyes, connecting under my nose. I sniffle the salty rain, slurping it up.

A soft hand touches mine. Lace has come to find me. She links our fingers and we touch heads, sprawling into a laughing star, suspended in the rain. Time loses meaning as the water melts around the shell of our bodies. The strands of our hair intertwine and, cheek to cheek, we breathe as one.

A scream overhead pierces the air as the seagulls protest the rain, fighting for empty space. The sky is dim enough to watch their flight free from the sun's glare. With their claws tucked under their tails, they glide, swimming in an expanse we'll never reach. As a kid, I used to lie down and imagine the ceiling's void as a stark, upside-down room that you entered by climbing over the doorframe. The gulls' sky is a sea of emptiness where they float in a mirror image of me.

Lace chokes on a wave and we surface together, the shoreline receding on the horizon as we drift softly, slowly away. She turns and breaks into a crawl to join the others. Her limbs cut the lake like scissors.

The sky grows dense and starts to bear down, so I dive to escape. I grab handfuls of the sandy bottom, releasing them to keep only the seashell debris. The scales cut my palms. I chew a fistful and they crunch in my molars. I'm a stingray.

I'm blinded underwater by the sediment and lake dirt suspended all around me. I merge with it in a plankton dance. When I come up for air, he's flying right overhead. Filthy buzzard, I'm not food for you yet.

They call me from the shore with a beer, but I drift a little longer, not ready to resume human form. My clothes are heavy, so I shed them to the endless lake, returning naked to my friends. I down my beer in one frothy gulp without a breath. Mel hands me another one, cold this time, that creeps into my guts like an octopus. Its tentacles invade my lungs and intestines, then slide farther down on the inside, gently fingering me. I throw myself on Mel, who wraps me up as I knock him to the ground.

Everything blends into one; Alexie's arms around Seth, Lace with Pete. We tangle together in a web.

Vicki's off on her own, teeth grinding.

—

We whine about the heat the whole way back, stuck in a traffic jam on the Don Valley Parkway. After what feels like forever, Seth finally breaks away and takes the exit under the bridge. We perk up when we realize what he's doing. He parks in a cloud of dust. One of us has to go down and check if the path is clear, and they cling to their doors, nominating me by default.

The gravel scrapes my calves all the way down the steep incline, and I struggle for balance, sending an avalanche of tiny rocks into the ravine. My feet catch in stray roots and beer cans. When I reach the water, I call up to them on the ridge that the path is clear. A fresh new rockfall cascades as they stumble their way down to the riverbank.

Obstructed by the Queen Street Bridge, the beach can't be seen from the parkway. It lurks beneath the road amid strewn drifts of litter. The bank is narrow, confined by concrete. Broken glass mixes with the stones and bricks on the apocalyptic embankment. The river breaks against it in a yellow foam so thick you could cut it with a knife.

Lace and Mel already have their clothes off and are making their way to the water, careful not to step on the debris. Alexie opens a beer and gets undressed too, playing with the rocks. I stay on my own. With my back against the concrete, I can almost touch the water with my toes; that's how tight the shore is. I crush the heels of my sneakers and kick them off. The water is hot like spit.

Between the cement slabs grow wild blades of grass, lapped by the river's slimy tongue. Lace and Mel are fighting over a floating grate, maybe part of a fence, overgrown with creeping weeds. More than half of it is covered in sludge, transforming its composition. Mel and Lace quickly lose interest and it floats off, bobbing lazily downriver on the weak current. The metal part has sunken, leaving only the grasses, streaking away in ribbons on the surface.

I strip off the shorts and T-shirt I got from Lace, the luxurious temptation of weeds and filth too great to resist. The river is thick, viscous, syrupy, and I float without trying. Plant life gathers between my toes, embedding in my body hair. I make a cup with my hands and scoop up a broth of putrescence. The water escapes my fingers, leaving only the silt, which I smear on my face and hair before taking off after the grate.

The current is slow, but the water's so dense, it carries me off. The breeze dries the muck on my face, turning it into a cracked mask. I glide on.

My head drains of thought. I am the current, the murk, the remains. A plastic bottle floats past as I drift on my back with my toes outstretched. My hair spreads like a corona around my face. I suck on a strand and close my eyes, moving my fingers down to find the creases, explore the folds. I pull my lips open, searching for the breach. Water flows in and out of me with the current, little waves probing my anus. I spread myself open wider, swallowing the warmth.

I slide my thumb and forefinger down around my clitoris and move to the river's pulse. My breath shortens. My feet sink and my mouth fills with water, the river's penance. I let it pull me down. Under the surface, there's just me and silence. Reaching behind me, I touch the slippery little rocks at the bottom. I catch onto them and interrupt my course, turning halfway, emerging to find myself downstream, a wave of plastic waste rushing against me. Just as I right myself, Seth pulls me out by my hair. I spit a mouthful of drainage in his face, but it doesn't crack his smug grin.

Our clothes stick to our wet bodies, and one of my sneakers got carried off. I climb up the embankment in my bare feet.

I didn't come.

❧ 4 ❧

THE BREEZE THROUGH the window hits my neck, shooting dust in the halo of my desk lamp. The room is black, with just my textbook in the slice of light and one chapter left to go. I've made pages of chaotic notes, hoping to at least memorize the ideas I can't understand. With just a few hours left, I try to thread them like beads in my head. But something's still missing. I know the definitions and formulas, the charts and statistics, schema and exceptions, but there's no depth to my understanding; it's all surface.

I switch off the computer and look at what I've written, following along with my finger. I make notes on top of notes, slowly linking links in tender sprouts of learning. But I know I have to stop. If I dig too deep, the whole structure will crumble. Nonetheless, I've made some headway. If I keep going I'll start questioning everything I've learned, so I close the book and stuff it into the mess of my bag, along with a handful of pencils.

The apartment is quiet, the three closed doors protecting their secrets. I don't know if they're asleep or out. As I pass through the kitchen, I slow down to test my resolve. Maybe I'll eat after I shower. Kill some time. Cheat my hunger.

The disinfectant smell from the bathroom reminds me it was Vicki's turn to clean. I lay out the pristine bathmat. In the hot steam, my skin emits a chlorinated vapour.

I lather the soap, releasing the foam between my fingers, down my chest and back. Rivulets dribble down my legs, catching on the hairs on my calves. I should shave, but neither of them left their razor in the shower. Ah well. I wash my hair instead, rinsing until my fingers squeak like rubber.

The water pressure is too weak. I need a lashing, a whipping, a stripping of my scales to leave me smooth and naked. A pressure to bend me double. Bow me down.

I reach out and quickly wrench the tap so that a freezing blast splits my back. I stand bolt upright, my stiffened neck pierced by the cold. My eyelids turn to hard, painful little shells. I endure it for another moment before turning off the tap. I wrap a towel around my waist. It's twenty-seven minutes after midnight. I brush my teeth: don't eat.

Blue light filters through the living room windows. I rest my forehead against the glass of the balcony door overlooking the garbage from the convenience store and shudder when my naked chest touches the cold surface. I take a step back. A man is out walking a tiny dog, his neck curved over his phone as he crosses the street without looking. There's a light in one of the apartments across the way, but I don't see anyone. My gaze drifts to the empty street.

A couple walks out of a house to my left. The woman lights a cigarette and sits down next to the man on the porch steps, tousling her wet hair with her fingers. They pass the cigarette back and forth, which must be a joint. They sit in silence, him looking at his feet and her watching something in the distance. Her gauzy peignoir drapes like a veil down the steps as she blinks slowly, distractedly. When she takes a drag of the joint, her lips hang open to release the smoke.

I wonder if I would have stuck with swimming if I'd been prettier. Plenty of us drop it in our teens, more interested in going out, shopping, boys … sick of the pool's captivity. For me, it was the only way to stand out. I was fast. I lost my virginity to a guy I met at a provincial championship in Waterloo who I'd seen at swim meets since I started. As a kid, he had freckles and his ears stuck out; as a teenager, a powerful neck and the shoulders of a champion. He still had freckles. In bed, like in the pool, he was supple, in perfect control of his body. I still run into him from time to time. He swims for UBC now.

The woman has pulled her hair back in a loose bun. They've finished their joint. The man looks angry. The woman stares up at me. It's darker here than outdoors, so I shouldn't be seen. I don't move. Her eyes scan my building, then away.

A puddle has formed at my feet. If I don't clean it up, it'll mark the floor. I spread it around with my foot to evaporate between the slats.

When I look back out, the couple is gone.

It's fifty-three minutes after midnight, according to the stove clock. I have to steal a few hours sleep from this night.

I push my unfolded wash to a corner of the bed and lie in the scent of the fabric softener, its sickly sweetness creeping over me. The sheets are cold, and my frozen body can't warm them. I curl up into myself, fighting the fear of insomnia. Don't think of the exhaustion, the fallout. I burrow in my spongy mattress, embedding myself in the worn sheets. If I move, I'll be exposed and have to start again. My hair saturates my naked pillow, my head resting on the stain left by all the other nights I've gone to sleep with wet hair.

∽ 5 ∾

I WOKE UP LATE and left without brushing my teeth. Now I run my tongue over their rough surface, struggling for the answer, scratching a canine with my fingernail. The question seems simple, but I feel like it's a trap and don't know which answer is right.

The amphitheatre is so big, the teaching assistant checking our ID cards has to zigzag kilometres to reach us all. The answer sheet takes up the whole table, which is welded to the chair. It's hard to concentrate with all the throat clearing, pencil scratching, and desk shifting. This doesn't look good. I force my focus to the page, shutting out everything else, a skill I've perfected. The noise disperses bit by bit and I finally settle in.

I blacken the boxes, creating a dotted path I hope

is right. They'll correct it by machine to ensure it's free from deviance. Each step out of line is a mistake. My form has to be perfect. As usual.

The room is half full when I pack up my things. A few students blow on their sheets, their eyes on the clock. I hand in my copy to a bored teaching assistant and walk out of my final exam, free. I have the whole summer ahead of me, but more importantly: France. I'd stopped myself from thinking about it, but now I can start making plans. I fly out Friday with Seth, Pete, Mel, Lace, and Vicky. Alexie didn't get picked. He said her Nationals scores were too low. As I walk out of the centre, I'm blinded by a sun I didn't know had risen. Broad daylight. Free from the constraints of school, I can fully embrace it. I amble home at a pace I rarely allow myself, the street vibrating beneath my feet as a new articulated streetcar grinds its way around a corner of rusted track. I let it pass. There's no hurry. Spadina smells like kebab. Farther on, it's glazed meat, steamed fish. I'll buy a mango later.

The Girondins meet is in Arcachon. I'll get to see the other Atlantic, the one where I've never swum. The more dangerous one. I can't wait to walk on that beach, to be right there and feel the sand between my toes. I look down at the dirty sidewalk of Spadina.

I take off my sneakers and socks. The concrete scrapes the bottoms of my chlorine-thinned feet, cutting my soles, stinging, and biting. I let it do its worst until its teeth grow dull with acceptance. Pulling back my shoulders, I straighten up and descend Spadina with a shoe in each hand, the way I'll dawdle through Arcachon. I'm already there in my mind. These pedestrians could all be naked if they didn't wear the burden of their day. I see them, but they don't see me. Their steps grow narrow, more precise. They seem to intermingle, moving forward, but also back. Nothing holds me here. My feet grip the concrete, ready to spring off somewhere else.

I'm home. I didn't buy a mango. The bottoms of my feet are black with filth, grit embedded in the cracks. Spadina was sandy.

Silence pushes out the walls, making the space feel bigger. I drop my bag in the hall and collapse into bed with the door open. A shroud of humidity seeps through the window I should have closed. Kneeling on my mattress, I brace against the bedding, but the window is stuck with coats of paint from a succession of tenants and won't budge. The woman next door is out smoking on her balcony again, alone this time. Crushed against my window, I watch her stare into the distance. We exhale together, long and careless. She's wearing a skirt hitched up around her knees with a knotted T-shirt. Alexie has the same kind of skirt.

I pull on the corner of my sweatshirt and tie it,

making a ball that reveals my waist. I drop back into the sheets and wonder if Alexie would let me borrow that skirt for Bordeaux. My half-packed bag sits in the corner. We don't need much, just the things on his list, like we're going off to summer camp.

The moisture sticks the sheet to my back as I catch up on hours of lost sleep, eyes half closed, not just from last night, but the whole semester. The dark mornings and kilometres covered. The time that splits into quarter-seconds on digital displays, on clock faces with sprawled hands, the endless accumulation of laps. I sleep the distracted sleep of the ambitious, afraid to slow down and trust comfort. But I finally succumb, rolling my stress into a pillow.

I sleep like the dead.

The sky darkens, and I sit up to watch the clouds pass. It'll be a quick thunderstorm. Drops smack the pane, splattering my exposed stomach. I don't bother trying to close the window. I extend my arm and try to catch the rain, the water trickling down to my armpit. I suck my fingers one by one, then my wrist, and fall back into the mattress. The rain bursts through and I stick out my foot. When the storm passes, turning to spittle, I stay in this strange position, wide open. Offered up.

∽ 6 ∾

SOMEHOW, I'M MORE exhausted now than when I went to bed. The alarm rang forever before I heard it. I could still sleep for hours, but missing practice is not an option; the whole team would pay. I have to pull it together.

From the bed, I drag on a top, sweatpants, and big socks to warm my stiffened body. It hurts to sit up. When the strap of my bag meets my shoulder, it awakens an old kink. I leave the house bent like a hook.

My knees creak, the gears blocking up with every step as I rheumatically approach the Athletic Centre. I push the turnstile, a winded crone.

In the empty locker room, I undress shivering, the effort making me feverishly sweat. I crawl into my bathing suit and the elastic invades my skin. As sole consolation, I wrap myself up and bury my nose in my towel.

When I pass through the chamber, I hope for a life force that doesn't come.

The pool seems too shallow and I can't do anything right; my strokes are weak and I swallow more water with every pull. I lose count of my lengths. When I go to turn, I can't resurface. My muscles seize and the water sucks me down, too heavy to bear. I stop fighting and sink, pulled to the dead abyss. My lungs burn as the water eats me from inside. Too weak to resist, let me curl up down there and quit. No more moving forward. I'm drained, alone, the liquid host bent on claiming me. My muscles are spent, the effort pointless. The surface has inverted so I don't swim to the edge, but the source.

My closed eyelids glow in the firelight burning on the pool's floor, and I plummet as it calls my name, swirling into the depths.

Then a jolt.

Something shakes me violently and I push at the arms that pull me me against my will.

My head hits the floor and his lips block mine in a painful mouth-to-mouth. People are speeding around me, next to me. I refuse their help. I can't take any more. Let me sleep.

I spew a mouthful of acid, unable to contain it. The cries I hear aren't mine. The whole team is gathered, their worried voices melding in a fog. I can barely breathe. They turn me on my side in lifesaving pose, and I curl up with my thumb in my mouth, sucking a lost childhood.

My fingertips probe the shapes of the tiles, tracing the familiar pattern now imprinted all over my flesh. I'm tattooed with ridges, my weight filling the cracks.

I'm a fractured doll.

Alexie frantically tries to wake me up, but he takes her aside, telling her I'm fine and to give her space.

I crumple on a faraway bench as practice resumes without me. He doesn't glance in my direction. I've let him down. I cough up failure long and loud, horking bile. My vision stays veiled by a gauzy black shield. I refuse to take part, curling up alone, dissolving in my shame. Holed up in an infectious cloud where I plan to stay.

They finish up without me. I stagger out when they leave, unsure I'll ever fit back in.

—

I can't afford recuperation time. I'll lose my Bordeaux spot if I miss even a minute. We all have to take the medical this afternoon.

My muscles and breath returned overnight, but a part of me stayed down there.

Slumped in the living-room armchair, I stare at the Christmas lights we never took down. I don't remember who put them up, but their hellish blinking hypnotizes me. A few bulbs have burned out. Wrapped around the non-functional chimney, the string throws a cold, useless glow.

I chew on a strand of my hair. I have to get ready, but the idea of standing makes me sick. My head is already spinning. The ceiling lurches and spins when I move. The vertigo lodges in my temple, my stomach, my fingers. Blow out my entrails, ransack my remains.

I've become one with the cushions, conquered by their softness. The sunken chair was salvaged from Lace's parents' house. They were going to throw it out. The canvas is worn, with stuffing seeping out. The shredded edges have gone dark and smudgy. It smells like fried food, onions, dust. The fragrance of Lace's childhood. It wears the scars of beatings and dried tears. She wanted to hang on to it as a memento of the misery.

We all came with our little bit of history, often in the form of furniture. The big carved wood table is Alexie's, covered in marks from forks and knives and burns. It bears the greasy veneer of candle wax, the edge tacky with endless coats of varnish.

The plastic chairs came from Vicky's basement. She lost her virginity on one of them.

The bookshelf is mine, still marked with skateboard

stickers, unreadable names on the shelves discoloured by trophy bases.

It takes a spring poking into my back to finally get me up, and I drag on yesterday's T-shirt and dirty jeans. I remember to put my vaccination record and a Gatorade in my bag before slamming the door I may or may not have locked.

——

The office is huge. Seth, Pete, Vicky, Lace, and Mel huddle together on the benches, silent, ridiculous, and scared. They didn't tell us what kind of exam to expect. I wait with them, bag between my feet, drinking big gulps of Gatorade. Our bottles of pee sit side by side in a basket. In the waiting room light, we're the colour of our samples.

There's a poster of a black forest across from us. Strange choice for a waiting room, a painted wood of dead fossils.

They call me first. I leave my friends without look-ing at them, following an obese nurse stuffed into her uniform. She points me to a seat in the sample lab. I'm terrified of needles, but I hold out my arm against a crowded shelf and look the other way as she manhan-dles me. There's a split in the leather chair where the fibres creep out, and I poke it with my finger when the needle goes in. She takes a few vials from me, having to retie my arm and swivel the needle to get the last two. I've dried up.

My elbow is already turning blue, an egg-sized swelling beneath my skin. She points me to a room where an open-backed blue hospital gown hangs. I wander out of the room, not sure where to go. My skin sticks to the plastic wall as I wait for them to come get me. I see them taking Mel into another room, pale and tame. He doesn't look at me as he follows the young intern.

A technician finally appears, guiding me to a completely dark examination room. She lays me down on a bed beside a sprawling monitor/screen configuration. She pulls up my gown, squirts gel all over my belly, and drags an ultrasound wand over it for fifteen minutes. Every image goes *pleep*. She places a triangular pillow under my hips, hitching them up. Without warning, she slides a probe inside me and digs around, making a deep, wet racket. She hits the end of my vaginal canal a few times. On the wall in front of me is a poster saying that technicians are prohibited by law to discuss test results. I let her explore.

Just as I'm starting to get dressed, she stops me. I still have to do an EKG and chest X-ray before I even see the doctor.

I'm covered in electrodes and tape. This time, the technician takes the time to explain the process, talking directly with me about my slow heart rate.

Now it's just my old friends the X-rays, of which I've had dozens. Wrists, ankles, knees, humerus, cubitus, they've all been fractured. They'll certainly see the scars. They dress me in the heavy lead apron, and the technician leaves the room to talk with the nurse, who comes back in to talk to me. They're not doing X-rays. The doctor will explain.

After hours of testing, we're back in the waiting room, all of us a little more humiliated and broken.

This time I'm last. The consultations go long and I catch myself dozing off sitting up. The sun is setting when they finally call me. Everyone has left—even the secretary has gone home. I must have fallen asleep. The doctor greets me wearing a Hawaiian shirt and flip-flops, like he's off to catch a flight. His office faces the examination rooms, and I follow him down a series of dark corridors. The room is luxurious, with two expensive chairs facing a glass desk, behind which he settles importantly. He assumes a serious look before opening my file. Something's not right. He starts out reassuringly. My heart, my lungs, my blood tests all show a healthy, athletic female. I'm in Olympic form. My little drowning episode was nothing more than exhaustion. I have to make sure to get enough rest.

I wait for the bad news. He directs me to an exam table I hadn't noticed at the other end of the room.

He gently lifts my T-shirt and palpates my stomach.

The embryo, he tells me, is still too small to be felt beneath the skin. But without question, it's there, and has been for close to eight weeks, according to the blood tests. I feel nothing. The news leaves me cold, but for a languor that blurs my edges. Obviously, this throws a wrench into my plans; I can't go to Bordeaux pregnant. Unless he doesn't record it in my file, that is. Which he's happy to consider. If I let him continue the exam.

His hands are on my breasts, under my T-shirt, massaging. My nipples get hard as he pinches the dark skin between his fingers and slips off my top over my head. Still holding me, he pulls over a rolling chair and undoes his pants. His erection pokes up from a dense forest of black hairs. He jerks off with his nose in my chest. His lips close around my nipples and he sucks them awhile, almost biting. He times the flicks of his tongue with his stroking rhythm, his breath cold on my belly. His teeth sting. He pulls hard on my breasts, his shaft slapping his hand. When he comes, he bites my enflamed areola.

I get dressed. He makes a note in my file and hands it to me without a word.

7

THE LAST WEEKS trickle by with the looseness of the season's end. Now that the competitions are over, a sort of haze has settled in. When practice gets out, we cut loose.

We said we'd meet in Kensington Market but didn't specify a location, so half the team didn't make it. I down my second IPA and Alexie is already talking too loud to Mel, who's draped on her shoulder, listening. I wore a skirt to try and look festive. The stubbly outgrowth on my thighs catches in the thin fabric. Behind us, two women drink white wine, perched forward at their table so they can hear each other. Lace is convinced I have to bring a box of condoms on the trip, because in France you can't buy them over the counter. I nod and agree, ordering another beer. My head is spinning and my stomach is heavy. The bar is hot. My glass leaves a puddle on the varnish, which I streak out with my finger as I listen to Lace.

The reclaimed barn wood walls reverberate with drunken echoes. The floor is covered in peanut shells. The laminated posters and menu have melted into the wood. It's supposed to look worn, familar. I dig a nail into the table varnish, creating fresh ridges. Lace thinks the French are perverts, but they're modest about it. The varnish in the knots of the wood is thicker and forms a glazed pool. I crush a few peanut shells, lick my finger to pick them up.

Pete wraps an arm around my waist and another around Vicky's neck. I squirm, but he doesn't let go. I give up. The beer is making me woozy. My mouth is salty and I feel nauseous, but my head has stopped counting and my gaze wanders. Lace, Pete, and the pool of varnish on the table all blend into one calming tableau that I leave unscrambled. I pick a peanut shell out from a canine and smile, at Pete, at Lace, at the table.

I lift the hair from my eyes with the splayed backs of my fingers and it falls back down. Lace appears beyond the shroud of my bangs. My eyes are slitted vertically, half-mast. I tuck my hair behind my ear and stay leaning on that palm. I drink sideways, dribbling on my shirt. My attention drifts in and out. I should have eaten. Pete slides his hand under my shirt, probably under Vicky's too. His fingertips brush my naked breasts.

My stomach warms up. I release my shoulders and smack my lips. The beer has calmed my hunger. I feel full. The cotton of my T-shirt falls over the outline of Pete's fingers.

I don't see Alexie. The two women behind her have finished their wine and there are three young guys sitting there now. I feel like I know the one on the left. Pete's hand moves up my skirt, and I decide to stand up and go to the bathroom. When I get close, I realize I don't know the guy, but he returns my smile anyway.

There's a long line for the women's washroom. I ignore the bunch of them leaned up against the wall, waiting, and go to the men's. In the mirror, my eyes are red and my lips are pale. My face is droopy. My hair, on the other hand, seems to have tangled itself upward. I pat it down with my hand, but it stays the same.

The guy I thought I knew is waiting for me outside the toilets. His hand is firm and damp. He takes me toward the back where they stack the empty beer cases and recycling. A breeze blows from inside the door, blowing my skirt, which his hands are already beneath. He gropes my buttocks, marvelling. He doesn't know any girls who swim. He's a good, greedy kisser, and holds a fistful of my hair as he enters me, his dominance gentle and complete. My body surprises him as he uncovers bits of me piecemeal, never all at once. He likes that I undress like this, prodding and tasting my chlorinated body. My shoulders intimidate him. He points at, then pinches them without venturing with his whole hand. He whispers that I'm beautiful. He's shorter than the guys I'm used to, and browner. I hold his torso with both hands, following the line down his stomach. He has dark hair, black in the dusky night. Its fullness is reassuring. He comes without me, then hands me his number, which I hang on to since I have no bag or underwear to put it in. He kisses me near my ear and leaves.

I wipe up the semen between my legs with the edge of my skirt and head back in to find my warm beer. Pete gapes at my return, sniffing me while still talking. He can smell him on me and is offended. I turn my back to him and order another beer, turning the phone number over in my hand. When I look over at the guy's table, he winks and smiles at me without opening his mouth. His eyes are almond-shaped, almost hooded.

I want to tell Alexie, but I don't see her anywhere. Lace either. Vicky is ready to go home and insists it's time; we fly out tomorrow morning. I slide my beer over to Pete and follow Vicky.

Kensington is cold. We walk arm in arm, weaving

over the foot-worn street. Cars are second-class citizens around here. We swerve diagonally to the opposite sidewalk, finding ourselves with a bunch of people we don't know. Someone takes Vicky's other arm, but I get her back as we reach our street. We say goodbye to the strangers like old friends, with just enough sense not to invite them up.

Barely through the door, we throw ourselves on Vicky's bed and fall asleep laughing.

Part Three

∾ I ∾

A BREEZE SENDS sand into my ears. It's already caked on the back of my head, in my eyelashes, my nose. I didn't bother with a towel, just laid right out on the ground. I stay on the surface and burn while the others swim a little way down the beach. I can hear them goofing off, boisterously free. I'll join them in a bit. I turn onto my stomach, lay my cheek down, and squeeze my eyes shut. I release handfuls of sand, kicking my feet as it rains down, tingling against my back and sunburnt thighs.

By the time I stop, I've burrowed a hole where I curl up, my eyes crusted with sand. The trench is shallower than I'd thought—just a few centimetres deep. The beach smells like warmth and iodine, blending with sunbeams. The fusing of opposites. I peer through the octagonal in my sand-caked eyelids, my tears sending brown streaks down my face, but there's nothing sad. It's my first time in France and if I could, I'd swallow the whole shore. Take it home with me. I roll in my burrow until it gets too scratchy, then, caked in sand and dust, I hurl myself in the ocean.

My thighs don't seize when they hit the cold. Submerged in the thick, salty sea, I thrash myself clean and emerge like new. I'm too fast for this water, the power of my strokes mismatched with the extra flotation, but my swim is festive, jubilant. A carnival crawl. My head is empty, my hair loose, my body bikinied. I'm normally strung up like a sausage. In the ocean, I can expand. The water is blinding, the natural rays bouncing off as it rebuffs them.

I swim my hardest, my longest, then, winded, I float. My body undulates with the curve of the waves. The sea is mine. I bob joyfully, eyes stinging with sand and salt. I shiver, but I stay. My flesh has no memory. Before, I was burning. Now, my teeth chatter.

I catch up with the rest of the team, who grab me because it's time to go.

I take a last look at the ocean and promise I'll come back tomorrow. I've taken some of the beach between my toes, but it dries too fast, and by the time I'm on the bus taking us back to the Pessac campus, it's all gone.

I sleep on the hot leather seat. The rest of them smell like seaweed, sun, and sweat. We've travelled back to our organic state.

When we stop at the campus, they have to yell to wake us. We've fused to the seats, melted into the window frames, coughing up salt. The bags at our feet have tumbled and their contents have scattered. We grab our own things and others', and climb down, hanging on to each other. We grudgingly split off to go to our dorms, using our free night to sleep. Enough freedom for one day.

—

The Girondins pool is outdoors. The surface, glazed like frosting, flows to the drain in three shades of blue. The shallow end is a light purple with a hint of yellow, and the deep end is marked by a dark-blue gradation, easing into green. All around the edge is light, but not white, more of a grey or an eggshell.

There's a pattern on the liner meant to mimic waves. It's distorted by the water, the sun forming diamonds just beneath the surface.

The mortar is rough against my soles, but as soon as the splashing starts, it'll get slimy.

I'm compelled to dive. My impact causes a few ripples that dissipate in the still, giant mass. The smattering of bubbles flattens by the time I'm halfway across.

A current spins out behind me as I kick, my feet drumming the surface.

The water slurps my shoulders, torso, and back in a big, wet kiss, bending my image into an ironic clone of the truth. I bow to its dominance and let it break me open. The water alone will have me.

There's not much time before the pressure catches up, so I seize the lull, gliding on without thinking. I wish I were naked, but at least my two-piece leaves my belly free. I do a few lengths of back crawl, not even trying to improve my sloppy technique. I want to see the sky. The sky. I never get this perspective. I take off my sunglasses and move at the clouds' pace. The sun is low and doesn't blind me. I feel the wind for a moment, but only just. My shoulders rotate in perfect time with the sway of my hips, undulating with amphibious curves. My limbs work independently, free from my will. I hand control to my reptilian brain and float aimlessly in my element, happy going nowhere. I swim in the lake, river, swamp, ocean. I am trout, I am swordfish, I am pike. My body is an unstoppable wave creating none. I want the pool to tilt sideways and dump into the river. Then I'd travel up it as a salmon, oblivious to the current. I want clean water, mineral, sedimented, with a murky bottom. I do some somersaults to forget I'm in a fishbowl, finding no treasure at the sterile bottom. Cursing my need, I surface and catch my breath. Amateur. Oh, to grow gills and escape, to the lake, the river, the ocean, the falls. Living bodies. But my waters are dead, antiseptic, gentrified. Later, we'll go back to Arcachon Bay, and I'll escape.

I'll quit bathing. My mouth will turn to marsh. I'll spread myself open and fill up with the natural stream. Impregnated by the sea, I'll be born again, amphibian, and I'll never go back to my bowl.

The others raid the pool and the water clears; my algae recedes and the mud washes clean. Their splashing has scared off the fish, their freestyle repelled the plankton. Chlorine regains control and I swim once again in formation. The ropes that keep me in my lane remind me to tighten my abdominals, broaden my shoulders, tuck my chin and dive. My muscles tense the way they know and perform as they've been trained. My speed doubles. My laboured huff is regular, regimented.

❦ 2 ❦

I HAVE A single room, with one twin bed facing a tiny sink, a few grey decals to liven up the wall, and a desk. Come September, some student will move in here for a year. They'll be Algerian, Russian, Moroccan, Sudanese, American. They'll be happy. A spot here at CROUS, with a flat sheet folded in a square to welcome them.

The room is bigger than mine back in Toronto. I haven't put anything away, I just dig for what I need and leave the rest strewn around. My toothbrush is in a glass on the sink. The toilets and showers are communal.

Practice this morning was brutal, leaving my muscles like torn asparagus spears. We have the afternoon off, but now we're useless. Just empty shells. A bunch of us wait for the electric tram to take us into town. Vicky is wearing a sheer dress that dances around her thighs. I'm wearing shorts and my pool sandals. We had fries and meatballs for lunch, and I still have the smell in my hair and bits of cartilage between my teeth that I pick at with my tongue. When the tram arrives, it's already packed. I thought our stop was earlier in the route. We squeeze in. I'm crushed against a girl whose feet I can see, but not her face. The skin of her calves is thin and white, like a jellyfish, the black hairs of her closely shaved legs like a contrasting connect-the-dots. Her flesh is plump and bloated like a drowned corpse. I know she's not pretty. Her chin's probably huge. Her warm body rubs up against mine.

The tram is completely quiet, travelling on new, unblemished rails. I'm waiting to hear the squeals, the familiar shuddering of the Toronto trains, but this one is noiseless. It has no soul, travelling like an electric eel.

The man in front of me gives up his seat to a drowsy child and her mother. The girl sleeps with her mouth pressed into her mother's arm and her eyes half-open. The woman wears hospital scrubs and has tired, empty eyes.

The tram stops swaying and continues in a straight line to Place de la Victoire. We push against the back door and tumble out to the sidewalk. They want to shop, get coffee, eat chocolate croissants, find a park, try the ice cream, visit a church. First, we eat.

There's no ice cream parlour in Place de la Victoire, just a Quick. But we find a bakery and some chocolate croissants, which we get all over our T-shirts as we wander up Rue Sainte-Catherine. At first, we don't venture into the stores around us. We recognize the products, but not the names. Etam. Bordelaise de Lunetterie. André. Kookaï. Galeries Lafayette. I look down at the bumpy cobblestones under my feet, like pebbles at the beach. The others finally start wandering in and out of the stores, but I stay on the shore. I have no money, and there's nothing I want. I close my eyes and watch the sun through my eyelids. They bought lingerie for Vicky, all of them going into the change room together and getting thrown out by the sales ladies. They're pleased with themselves. Pete holds the back of my neck all the way to the shops at Alsace-Lorraine, where we get strawberry-vanilla-swirled ice cream in cones that taste like cardboard. We take pictures to remember the ice cream and Vicky's dress. We lick our sticky wrists. I suck the ice cream out of my cone, wearing the tip on my tongue like a pointy little hat. Seth laughs in my hair.

At Place de l'opéra we don't know where to go, bumping into each other before coming to stand at the big, empty fountain. We saunter off, wandering instinctively along the Garonne. The road is busy, with shiny little cars weaving around each other much too fast. We reach the water's edge, relieved. Before us is the Miroir d'eau, a few centimetres deep, stretching across the immense surface, reflecting the Place de la Bourse and the quay. We blend in with the kids, splashing our clothes and bags, except we're louder. Vicky does cartwheels. I pretend I'm swimming. Pete tries to skate. The reflecting pool illusion entertains a disparate, serious crowd, and they don't take long showing their disapproval. Too noisy, too big, too Canadian. We don't care. The city smiles, even if its residents don't. I sit down on the edge to catch my breath, facing the Garonne. The quays are shaded in the afternoon sun, and the passersby, less numerous now, make their way to the patios for cocktails.

Seth sits beside me and lays his heavy arm around my shoulders. I catch his hand and set it down beside me. The mud-brown river flows between the arches of the Pont de pierre. The streetlights have come on too early, but we'll need them before long. Seth slides his hand between my thighs. I get up and take a few steps on the smooth promenade. The horizon is spiked with metal anchors they could dock hundreds of boats with. *Have they?* I wonder. I lose my footing on the rounded lip and nearly fall in, then step back flat on the ground to get my balance. The metal warms my back.

A driftwood limb snags in the branches ahead, then some grass in the driftwood, creating a little dam. The water is thick and filled with algae. It must be filthy to swim in. You'd be fighting it like quicksand, the killer liquid dragging you down.

Pete runs up childishly behind me, and pretends to push me in. I don't laugh. My mind is still in the gooey river. Now I'm in a bad mood and don't feel like going for drinks, but I put on my sandals and follow, sneaking looks back at the black Garonne, where I heard the suicidal cries of the drowned.

3

THE POOL HAS never looked so beautiful. I've only seen it cyan, not indigo. The moon's reflection alone distinguishes it from the rest of the scene. The edge feathers into the shrubbery, extending the little wall into Pessac. The town's shredded edges enclose the water. The pool doesn't see me. I am the offence in the shadows. We're not supposed to be here.

The others take turns scaling the wall, filling the night with their muffled laughter. The surface vibrates with their landings, raunchy and drunk. I mess up a dive from the three-metre board and explode in bubbles of laughter underwater, coughing my way to the surface. Seth does one reckless jump after another, swimming past us over and over. Lycra-free, we do what we want, our flesh white like babies, our private parts riotous.

Vicky catches her breath clinging to my neck, driving her nose into my ear as she kisses me. The boys are doing tricks, showing off for the Bordeaux girls who can't understand their vulgarities. They're the American Boys. Those girls don't need to learn their language; they'll talk with their bodies. Vacation friends. A French guy has taken Vicky's place, whispering kisses and feeling me up. I pry free and go do a few lengths, then slow down, drifting as the others get louder. I float, cradled in their waves, caught up in the stars. There are no stars in Toronto; here, they perforate the sky. I lose myself, floating in a black water reflection. With my ears submerged, I don't hear the noise die down or the sound of them getting dressed and leaving.

I float with my eyes open to the void, my back settling into the calmed surface until my foot grazes the edge and stops my meandering glide. Curtailing my fugue. My muscles tense on contact in arrival reflex and prepare to take off to nowhere. When I remember there's no race, I soften up, aware now that I'm alone. They've gone back to their rooms, or out to party, indulging their needs in whatever way. I launch into an easy front crawl to cut through the night. I could stay out here until morning. After a few more joyful strokes, I plunge feet first until I touch the bottom, rubbing myself on its roughness, clutching it as my buoyancy tries to lift me. I release all my air to gain some depth. To sink completely, crushed by the liquid weight. To stop this fight.

The water's texture turns heavy now, sedimentary, and invisible plankton emerge to greet me. Beneath the surface, I spin, pinching the blackness between two fingers, rolling myself like in a sheet. I open my mouth to swallow the indigo, excavating space inside. I'm done with the surface, but it still pulls me. The water hangs on too. I kick it away, it grabs me back, I whip it with my arms, it closes up around me. So I give up, capitulate to outdoor forces.

The air has cooled.

That's when I see them. They didn't leave. Off in a dark corner, they're exchanging bottles, joints, kisses. I join their little crowd with just my naked arms for cover. I get my lips on a bottle and a boy, and shiver as I haul on a roach. It's us now. The Bordeaux kids have gone off to find fun somewhere else. Seth and Pete are stacked against Vicky, who's asleep. I burrow in.

The night turns white, then morning.

I wake with Seth's hands on my head. He tells me to close my eyes as he pushes two fingers inside me, and I open right up. In the show he's casting, I'm the water, and he's asked permission. Just a fish headed back downstream. I let him go on without complaint. He puts a finger to my lips and beckons Pete, who assumes his position while Seth gropes my breasts, pushing my back into the concrete. They take turns swimming inside me, but I feel like I'm drowning. Vicky opens her eyes and stirs limply but doesn't react. She sees but does nothing. Leaning on one elbow, she gazes into the distance. I sink deeper, flapping my feet and arms with all my strength. I want to get up, but they hold me down before abandoning me to silence.

—

The orange-grey morning brings out the team. I didn't go back to my room. My head is pounding from the booze and I'm the only one left from last night's trespass. The rest of them ran off, leaving me to take the fall, like I broke into the pool by myself. I glare at them, but they stay mum, not about to take the hit. So he levels his rage at me; I don't know how lucky I am, I have no respect for myself ... He bellows, disgusted, and no one steps in. He shakes his finger at my nakedness, my degeneracy, my excess, before banishing me to the locker room.

My friends' semen drips down the inside of my thighs. The pain is so pervasive, I can't even tell where it's coming from. I throw up, but nothing comes out. It's stuck to my insides. I choke it down and reach for my tightest, most uncomfortable bathing suit, the one that splits my crotch, my shoulders, my chest. The fabric of misery feels right.

I line up for the starting block behind one of the Bordeaux girls. He's talking with the other coach, a woman with very short hair and shoulders like a quarterback. The lessons today are new, Olympian, with technique swapped for brute force. He explains how your kick starts in your shoulders, your strokes in your legs, and everything works together—including the team. I dive in. Last night is a stone I've swallowed that sinks me, ready to burst through my stomach. It's too heavy. I double my effort, beating the water top speed, escaping with my life. The wall comes too fast, and I turn, start back, covering length after length in my fury. I exhaust my anger until I've lost the strength to even feel it. Breath doesn't help, so I push it from my lungs. My starved body is streamlined, stretching out so I can touch both sides. I fill the space. I am the pool.

When I finally surface, I'm clean. Polished to a shine. I've washed off the night. The pulse vibrates in my wrists, ears, stomach, neck, back, throat. Blood burns in my veins. I throb rhythmically, peaceful and blue.

He gives me a smile I've never seen on him, showing me the clipboard after he's held it up for the Bordeaux coach. His voice is uncharacteristically soft, as he pulls me by the hand from the pool to parade me through the crowd. I am rapturous.

Pete and Seth are filthy specks; useless, nonexistent, smeared on the sole of my foot.

4

THE SHEETS ARE WET. I wake up when I feel the slime on the backs of my thighs. I haven't had my period in months, maybe years, but that's not what this is; there's way too much blood, and it's not stopping. I'm emptying out. Evacuating. A pain shoots through my lower back; contractions shred my abdomen. The suffering feels good. I pull off the bedding and use it to wipe myself, wrapping it around me for a dazzling stumble down the hall to the bathroom. The ceiling twirls and I lean against the wall for support, focusing on my steps. I press down each foot and anchor it to the cold ground.

The dorm halls are empty. I didn't check the time. When I get to the bathroom, I remember I didn't bring tampons and wrap myself back up to go to see Vicky.

Everything is brighter in her room. She's lined products up on her shelves and hung up her clothes, the right shoes arranged beneath them. She says she wasn't asleep; she was working out on a bath towel. I can take the whole box of tampons. She has more, even though she doesn't get her period either. I take the box without thanking her. She didn't say a word about my bloody sheets.

The tampon feels like an icepick going in. I gasp for air and collapse on the tiles.

A cloud like a soft fog forms around me as I start to hallucinate, conjuring a beach at low tide with children splashing in the puddles. The sand, cut with grey channels, snakes along, the ghosts of shadows blending with a too-low horizon. The sky and sand merge, flooding each other, their edges lost in the fog. They play together, digging caverns in the soaked ground. I am the children, the sand, and the fog, without distinction. I know the dull, grey feeling, the colour of memories, forgotten photographs. No one minds the rain when there's no such thing as bad weather.

I only realize I'm crying when someone knocks on the stall door. I'd been rustling my dirty sheets in my sleep. My cheek rests on the cool freshness of the toilet base. The pain has passed and I can stand up. I leave my nest behind me, ignoring their questions. They can make up whatever gory tale they like.

I keep my towel around my waist to hide the inevitable leak. The Bordeaux coaches have put on bathing suits to demonstrate the exercise they're teaching us. He has too, for the sake of appearance. He almost never gets wet. The technique they've developed was created by a computer, and the first thing they tell us is that it's designed for men, not women. The feminine form is too curvy to adapt. It's up to us to adjust.

The freezing water stops the hemorrhaging. Temporarily. When I dive, a lacy string of blood floats out behind me, breaks up, and dissolves. The cramp moulds itself with the effort. My heart rate speeds up until I can feel it in my stomach. My swim is a slapping dance. I can hear the muted rhythm of the liquid music. I execute the jerky, foolish new technique with my awkward body, knowing it's a power I have no choice but to master.

A giant girl from the Bordeaux team swims ahead of me, her muscles short and compact. Her enormous thighs form waves under her skin. Her shoulders are as wide as a bridge, her feet spread out like flippers. She doesn't wear a bathing cap on her shaved head. I swim along in her whirlpool, upstream. I don't know her name, but I know her times.

We're not built to evolve in the water. We're not fish,

but liquid in the liquid, an oil that resists on the surface, insoluble. I picture myself as aqueous, turning malleable and infinitely supple to slip in and out of the periphery.

I can't get it right, which frustrates me. My strokes are warlike and ungainly. I try and apply what I learned, but it all comes out wrong. He slaps his palm against the water to stop me mid-length—like I knew he would. My heart thumps back up my throat from the effort. He's crouching, backlit against the sun so I can't make out his face. The brightness burns my retinas and I squint at him so hard my view goes vertical. I catch my breath. His hair is vibrating in the light as he shakes with rage. He doesn't need to talk; his body says it all. I think he's overreacting—I wasn't that bad. He hauls me out of the pool and I stumble in the drain, his words striking like a hammer, each insult more brutal than the last. I don't even bother getting up, just lie there like a slug on the edge. Everyone around stops what they're doing to witness my destruction. I find my feet at last and lift a palm to respond. When he hits me, I'm already beaten.

I don't see the others come running over, but I hear the commotion from beneath the surface. They take him away and offer me a towel that I refuse. I'm not hurt. Everything's fine. I get back out and try to make light of it, ready for more. Their worry turns to shrugs as he takes his place at the far end of the lane and our eyes meet coldly, my cheek still numb.

5

PRACTICE STARTS LATE this morning, but he wants to see me. I brush my teeth and pull my hair back. Vicky lent me her skirt, but I don't wear it.

There's no office here, so I have to go find him in the breakfast room.

He tells me there are certain tensions destroying my energy, my excessive appetites are ruining my performance. My mind is elsewhere when all I should be thinking of is swimming. He has to rehabilitate me, it's part of the training. He'll take it on himself to release me gently from my indulgence, since it's his job to protect me from myself. And to do that, he needs to know me inside and out.

At the next table, a couple is fighting as they gaze into

the bottom of a glass, the woman stirring her straw in the syrup to release the Perrier bubbles. I do what she does.

There's an outing scheduled this afternoon to the Dune du Pilat. He suggests I stay in town with him for a session instead, but I'm dying to climb that dune and I insist. He reveals a canine in his sneer as he tells me to go, dismissing me with a wave of his hand. He doesn't apologize, likely expecting me to. I won't.

The bus stops under the pines and we sink into a prickly layer of golden needles. We left our sandals scattered under the seats; we'll walk the Landes barefoot. Mel takes Vicky's hand and I catch up with Lace. Seth and Pete take off, running like idiots. The Bordeaux team came too. Everyone loves Pilat.

The forest smells like sap and red sugar, a sticky smell, hot and round like resin. In its shade, we can almost forget the heatwave. We walk on in the cool dampness, the canopy of pines hiding the sky in a coniferous ceiling. We continue with our noses in the air, an uncharacteristically respectful silence. The forest lets us admire it, barely ruffled by our fascination. Branches crack under our crunchy steps until a breeze reveals the dune, luminous on the horizon. Our awe for the pine forest turns to excitement for the sandy expanse. We sprint for the ramp we're not going to use, aiming for the virgin incline.

At the dune's foot, the sky is obscured and there's

only the mountain of sand. My entire foot sinks into the mass, soft as dust, whose swirling clouds catch in Mel's hair, tousling his dense curls. He looks so young in the reddening sun. The light stops to play on his rounded cheeks, sparkling off his too-clear eyes, too-white teeth, too-browned skin.

Seth and Pete have already taken off their shirts and are rolling in the sand like puppies, falling down more than they climb up. Clinging to each other, their bodies meld indefinably, hugging, wrestling. Their friendship is a battle. They've never left boyhood.

Vicky is almost at the top while the rest of us have only climbed a few metres. She's just a fine line, unbroken in the distance. Her outline is distorted by the heat, a flaming mirage.

I don't see Lace, who's no longer holding my hand. I don't remember letting go.

The sand burns and I hop from foot to foot. It's the kind of heat you can drink like a syrup, coating your eyes and throat. It smells like hot carbon, marine sap, almost sexual, like warm skin. There's an iron taste in my mouth.

The dull, round grains slide between my fingers, leaving only a precious quartz residue in my palm. A gust of dry air strikes and soothes me at once as I watch the dunes stretch on forever in sensual curves, like a mineral coating. I melt into the surface, insignificant.

A man's voice calls out, then fades in the cries of

seagulls and children. It's a happy crowd, like rowdy schoolkids, drunk with the sun.

Seth, Mel, Pete, and Vicky tackle me, but I can't see Lace. The flat ocean at our feet is consumed up the middle by a sand bar. The earth reigns here.

Seth pulls some bottles out of his bag, and Pete, some pills. I take a few gulps of wine before dissolving the pill on my tongue. My next medical is a month away; there'll be no trace. The setting sun falls on Mel, whose skin has turned to coral. Mine is caked with sand stuck to the sweat. I inhale deeply, the smell of ocean and iodine chasing my migraine.

Under the influence now, I see hints of purple in the water, scarlet in the sand. The ocean peels away in strips. My vision is hatched. The world around me splits into fragments so I can see all its strata. Faces look eternal, like babies and seniors at once, like I've known them as both. Vicky's thin cheeks fill out, then crease into hideous wrinkles. Seth turns grey. I down the rest of the bottle. It's time to go.

A chill runs down my spine when we realize Lace isn't on the bus. Despite our insistence, the driver won't wait. The Bordeaux team is suffocating and wants to shower. She'll have to figure it out on her own. Under the seat, her sandals stir when the engine starts, then slide a few seats back.

∾ 6 ∾

THE SCREEN BREAKS DOWN my movements. My body is just a set of lines, my joints marked by circles. The computer has skinned me in a striking technological display, pivoting my body any which way to see my technique from all angles. The team watches me, their guinea pig. A dotted outline charts my direction so far as to predict my next mistake. The vectors are as clear as the errors. I'm exposed, more naked than ever.

My fingers tremble slightly.

I pull myself from the image to study it with the rest of them. I'm not concerned about the joints; I look at the lines and try to straighten them. Their corrections don't matter. My pelvis is always too high and breaks the horizontal, explaining the weakness of my kick. It's easy to forget the extremities.

One of the Bordeaux girls is doing her hair during the explanation, tirelessly dragging a square wooden brush through bleached-blond strands that tear away with each pass.

Vicky is putting on moisturizer. Lace still isn't back. He doesn't seem to have noticed she's gone.

A flock of seagulls fights viciously overhead, flapping their wings, releasing a shower of white feathers on us and the pool's surface. We stop and watch, unable to tell what they're fighting about. They fly apart, regroup, then attack again, their shrieks shattering the heat. Through cupped eyes, we watch their orange beaks squabbling bright against the sky. The boys imitate their squawks, adding their own noise to the already absurd cacophony. Someone throws a rock and they fly off somewhere else, leaving us with just the sound of water slopping slowly in the drain.

The gurgling of the pool makes me hungry. There's a gap between my stomach and the creased fabric of my suit. I pull my knees close to my chest to squeeze the cramp.

The coaches disperse, their red shorts little dots at the edges of the pool as they stand sentinel. He positions himself at the end of my lane, his lips forming a silent litany. Lyle. I can feel his eyes on me when I swim, but I see only the bubbles from my arms and those around me. The water is full of air. I'm a perfect line, free from rounded surfaces, my posture corrected, my trajectory perfect. I drill through the water as the resistance melts away.

———

I add a little water and the pastis clouds over, turning white. The opaque liquor spreads in milky waves. I make a little whirlpool with my spoon and lick it off, the anise liquid coating my teeth. I drink in tiny sips, letting the floral notes expand on my tongue. The licorice makes my mouth water with its ripe, grassy aroma.

The red-and-white stripes of the terrasse awning colour our faces. Two bearded French boys have joined us, Arnaud and Colin, or Quentin, I don't remember. The one whose name I've forgotten has long, dark eyelashes, dense like the woods, overgrowing his ocean-coloured eyes. I smile lazily from the pastis.

The alcohol courses through my spine, numbing my shoulders. Vicky is wearing a fitted yellow top with a white edge that might be a bikini top. Her tiny breasts are crushed, poking through the fabric. All eyes are on her.

With a cigarette between her lips, Lace pushes through the crowd of servers. But it's not her anymore. Something has changed in her movements. She collapses next to me, buries her nose in my neck and says nothing. I hand her my glass, which she downs in one gulp. I finish her cigarette, my breathing slowing, calming down; now that she's here, I can exhale. She puts her hand up my shirt and rests it on my rounded belly. I stroke her hair to smooth her furrowed brow.

The table is laden with our orders, fries with mayonnaise, magrets de canard, foie gras, gizzard salad, sausages, baked chèvre, tomatoes with mozzarella, sardines in oil, steak tartare, all the forbidden delights glisten on our greasy lips. Pastis turn to glasses of woodsy red, washing down the salt with wine. The French boys order more bottles and loosen their belts. I wipe my fingers on the tablecloth, laughing boozily with the rest of them. The boys scrape their plates, Seth licks a bowl. Draped over our chairs, we finish the bottles.

I don't know who pays.

We stumble toward the Place des Quinconces, where there's a fair underway, a sparkling white ferris wheel floating in the indigo sky. Seduced by the lights, we stagger on. The fairground smells like deep fryer and sugar.

The area is packed with game booths, caravans, and rides. Long black electrical cords snake across the ground, every surface sparkling with excitement. A wine-filled crowd cavorts in the chaotic space between temporary stands.

Behind the dirty glass of a pushcart, a woman sells tickets. We give her a wad of money and get a roll to share. We divvy them up and go off, each with our own strip.

My hands stick to the grimy metal safety bar that Pete pulls down in front of me before the ride takes off, trying and failing to light a joint at the same time. Our cars soar into the sky and we look out briefly over the Rue de la Garonne before plunging to the ground. I quake from head to toe in a cold, nauseous sweat. My mouth fills with spit and I drool over the side, a string hanging from my lip. Pete wipes my mouth with his thumb, smiling. I press myself against his chest. He kisses the top of my head.

The ride stops and I throw up next to our car, sneering at the attendant.

The boys want to try the pork belly sandwiches, strips of oily pork served on a baguette with mustard, sauerkraut, and fries right on the bread. We wash them down with an acidic Basque wine that burns my throat. The delicious grease drips down my neck, staining my shirt. A breeze lifts the flaps of the awnings as the night dims the fairground tones.

A woman with wild hair sits on a folding chair telling fortunes. Beside her is a patio table draped in coloured cloth, holding a little sign with her prices. Lace drags me by the elbow at a gallop. She sits in the empty chair and I stand beside her. The woman takes her hand, gently smoothing the creases. In an improbably accented broken French, she tells her about children, a great romantic disappointment … then she stops and looks deep in Lace's eyes. Her lips tremble. She returns Lace's hand after touching each of her chewed nails. She sees a great victory at the end of a great test. With both hands in her wooly hair, she says she feels an apprehension she can't name and suggests that Lace steer clear of animals. Her bushy brows knit for a moment, then she asks for the money to end our session. We stagger away, the alcohol not sitting right. Lace waves happily to the woman, who doesn't wave back.

Right next to her is a stand where they make candy by stretching long strings of taffy on hooks. Thick cables the size of a human arm thin out into tendrils, and a woman folds the shining, satiny ribbons. Repeating the motions like a machine, she creates long white, red, and yellow strands that intertwine without blending, then cuts them off into little candies the size of dice, setting them to dry on a sheet before wrapping them in cellophane. A child rams into me to buy some. I don't budge.

∾ 7 ∾

I'M SUPPOSED TO meet the others at Place Saint-Michel at noon to go to the antique market, but first I have a session in his room. The staff dorms are bigger than ours, the high ceilings brightening up the halls. Behind the doors, I can hear breathing, one-sided telephone conversations. A plant dies in a pot off in a corner and a vacuum blinks, unseen. His door stands open for me.

He's sitting on the ground on a cocoa mat, meditating. I watch quietly. He knows I'm there but doesn't react. The bed, sink, and desk are in the same triangular configuration as my room. A few bananas lie on the table. He holds out a hand for me to join him on the rug, and I sit opposite him in lotus position. He places his hands flat on my knees and gestures for me to do the same with mine. We synchronize our breathing to reach the same depth. He doesn't give me any powder. The oxygen intake makes me lightheaded. He covers my mouth, so I breathe through my nose.

The skin of his hand smells rancid, oily. His fingers cover easily more than half my face.

The cocoa threads prickle my thighs, and I focus to ignore the itching. He doesn't seem inconvenienced, still completely immersed in his meditation. His eyelashes, awfully dark for someone so fair, create a veil like a fan on his cheek. His lowered chin casts a shadow on his neck. He has a dimple that I can't see from this angle, but I know it's there.

He starts the humming, a deep, guttural sound at first, coming from deep inside him without moving at all.

The room smells like bananas, the fragrance sweet, green, disgusting.

Next comes the chanting. Lyle. He rolls his consonants, moving his tongue. I fight the urge to throw up. The heavy smell of the bananas is making me sick. I gulp down bile.

My seat bones press into the hard rug, the discomfort making me arch my back. I shift position slightly.

He chants. Lyle. His body vibrates, rumbling with the noise. I open my eyes. On the other side of the walls comes the sound of conversations and TV. The banality of the place hits me like a revelation. The unmade bed, the yawning suitcase. His melody hits a comical tone.

I push his hand away. Overcome with nausea, I stand against his resistance and for a second, he wonders what I'm doing; he's never had to use force. The brutality has always been consensual, and refusal wasn't an option. I had to face facts, face him, submit to the training. His training.

It's not me there for the rest of the session. Someone else absorbs, accepts, receives, while I stare at the bananas that blacken as I watch.

—

I linger for a long time on the arid campus with its burnt lawn. The trees produce no shade and there's nowhere to hide, so I keep to the molten concrete. I could go to my room, but for what? I drop into a seat at the tram stop.

There are caravans parked in the open field across the way. Smoking black trash bins produce an acrid, frying stink. Barefoot children chase a skinny dog across the sand. In the distance, their mothers stir giant pots. The Roma are blocked from the campus by a crumpled fence, which they use as a clothesline to hang their wash, sheets and faded tablecloths in a mosaic brought to life by the wind. From my room at night, I hear them making music.

I pull my knees to my chest, sweat forming where my skin meets. The tram to the centre of Bordeaux is almost empty, so I take up two seats. The unconditioned air is stifling in the car, so dense I could chew it.

The trip seems short. I must have dozed off. I take Rue Renière to where Place Saint-Michel widens before me. The antique market is closed. The vendors have loaded up their dusty crates, leaving behind just shelves and garbage. I wander through the remnants, empty boxes, utensils, fabric, and wrappings. Under a newspaper, I find a shred of lace and tuck it in my pocket.

Shielding my eyes with my hand, I look for my friends but don't see them. A gothic cathedral bell tower looms overhead, not attached to a building. It reigns unassisted, with the basilica set off to the side. The spire is pointed, decked with flowers blackened by pollution. A little crowd gathers at its base.

I take a walk around the cafés, but don't recognize anyone. I end up sitting at one, where they serve me a mint tea I didn't order. It's boiling, excessively sweet, with pine nuts rolling around at the bottom. Exquisite. I burn my mouth in tiny sips.

Some robed men pass by carrying waxed canvas bags, stuffed with groceries. A bunch of boys, smoking and roughhousing, fill the square with passing laughter.

A woman scolds her child. Tourists photograph an inconsequential tree. Two trucks get stuck in a narrow laneway, and the drivers get out to fight. Everyone stops to look. Yelling and waving, they point at the source of their fury, shouting themselves hoarse. With nothing resolved, they get back in and drive off, a cloud of black smoke in their wake.

My table is sticky. I stir a syrupy puddle with my finger, wiping my hand on the side of my chair. A couple of pigeons pick at crumbs on the ground.

Suddenly, my chair rears back and I almost fall over. Mel laughs his head off and sets me upright as the others take over the rest of the seats, knocking the table. My tea goes everywhere.

At the antique market, Pete and Seth bought a couple of hideous old dolls. Both faded blond, they have big, empty eyes, tiny mouths, and ridiculous pink cheeks. One is wearing a bonnet. Seth lifts up the dress of his doll to show us the dirty lace underpants beneath. Their shoes are painted right onto their feet. They sit the dolls in their laps and grunt, pretending to fuck them.

I light the cigarette Lace hands me.

8

I SINK MY HANDS in the muck, sliding the weeds between my fingers. I wish I never had to surface. I catch my breath for a better dive, clutching the grasses to stay under longer, and even lie down for a bit. The Dordogne is calm as a lake, the vegetation only stirring in the stagnant water when I do. No life swims around me, just a hanging green plankton. My eyes can open down here without burning.

I spin and do somersaults underwater, making myself dizzy. I'm covered in mud, rolling in the murky depths. My hair catches in the reeds as it brushes past, and I peel the strands, braiding them. A few of my bubbles rise to the surface. I grab the mud in a final resistance, but the strain in my chest is too great and after a quick panic, I rise for air.

I emerge, muddy, licked by the river's tongue. The mud clings to my body hair and stuffs my bathing suit, a mass collected in my crotch. I get dressed without drying off, sticking my shirt to my torso.

The Bordeaux team wanted to show us their river. On the rocky shore, I lose myself watching the canoes float lazily past. Old people paddle their inflatable boats without technique, their eyes hidden by fishing caps.

The rocks on the scrubby, unwelcoming shore dig into the soles of my feet. I step over driftwood and duck under branches, disturbing a grass snake that slithers into the woods bordering the water.

At first, I mistake him for a shrub, but then he moves toward me, ungainly body swaying, claws grasping the stones' edges. He bows by way of invitation and I caress his bald head, stubbly like shaved pubic hair, the skin folding in familiar contours under my fingers. He lowers down, offering himself for tenderness, and his beak tip pokes at my thigh, his big naked neck on my hip. He's gotten skinny. I wonder if he's mad that I've been neglecting him and stroke his long wings apologetically, the veins protruding over fine membranes of cartilage. My hand roams over his bumpy spine, taking the weight of his pain. His cool skin warms against my legs and the chill penetrates me, the heat transfusion leaving me listless. I swallow a cramp. When he's sucked all my energy, he releases me. And I join the others.

The air has cooled down. My hair dries in clumps as the water of the Dordogne laps against the shore in tiny waves, soothing me as I lean into a snoring Seth. The soft fur beneath his belly button is like a sweet little meadow on his otherwise hard body. I cuddle up against his warm skin. In his sleep, he puts an arm around my waist and pulls me closer. I'm aware of my skin's thickness, of little bulges that might gross him out. I take a deep breath and suck in my stomach, pushing out my ribs. I play with the knot of his bathing suit, pulling the string, trapping my hand under the elastic. His stomach growls beneath my ear and the sound of his hunger lulls me to sleep.

———

I effortlessly match Vicky's speed in the next lane, driven by the boost of energy from something swimming inside me. Vicky stops mid-lap and hangs on to the side, watching dumbfounded. I make a wide turn, gaining a few metres underwater before surfacing with a clear lead. At the end of the two hundred metre, my heart pounds in my neck, my temples, my stomach.

He saw; I can tell by the faint smile in the hollows of his cheeks.

I climb out of the pool in a single bound, ready for more. For a while, I feel I could have breathed amphibiously, in uninterrupted breaths, as though through a straw. The sense of power is intoxicating. I can't be drowned.

I absorb his words incuriously, not even listening. My body and mind are separated in a sort of trance, one that makes me cover kilometres in a single breath, and I'm troubled for a moment by the idea that I'll never pull the two sides together.

One of the Bordeaux boys congratulates me with a wink and a pat. I giggle. Algae grows wild in my stomach, lichen between my toes, sediment in my mouth.

❦ 9 ❦

THEY FEED US lunch and dinner at the residence cafeteria, but we're on our own for breakfast. There's a communal kitchen we use in the mornings. Every room has a little fridge, but the dishes are in the kitchen, as well as cupboards where food disappears the moment you leave it. There's a coffeemaker too. It didn't take us long to start hiding our cookies in our desk drawers.

The sink fills up as fast as the cupboards empty, and the dirty dishes belong to no one.

At my table, two sleepy students burn their throats on little gulps of coffee. I drink mine from a glass I can only hold for a few seconds, since there are no more cups. I'm out of milk and the sugar has disappeared, so I have to drink it black, which makes me queasy.

We don't talk, our puffy eyes fixed on our undrinkable coffee. I'm hungry. I brought some protein powder, but the mixer is in the sink. I let my stomach knot itself before I decide to clean the pitcher.

I pull out the mixer from the clamour of dishes. The sponge is at the bottom, and I tunnel in the filth to find it. A thick dried crust clings to the container's edge. The worn sponge is no match for it. I add soap and foam the oily water, splashing as I scrub. The crust grips the plastic. I scratch at the softening debris with my nails, food slithering under them, the slime pulling free in strips. The smell of garlic and rust rises from the marshy sink. The drain is plugged with muck and I grope around the swamp, a dirt ring forming around my wrists; the more I clean, the dirtier I get. I pick the sponge back up and start furiously scrubbing. Happy with the pitcher, I rub at a plate until the fake porcelain shines. I empty the water and start over, scouring a casserole dish, lids, glasses, spatulas, cups, knives. Nothing escapes. My skin wrinkling, I splash everything in sight. My clothes are soaked and a puddle forms at my feet, drops cascading from my cheeks, my hair. When the sink is finally empty, I scrub the bottom with steel wool, slicing my fingers in a hundred little cuts. I squeeze in a load of soap and foam it up. The steel wool scrapes my palms, my arms. My nails rip free. I add more soap and plunge myself in the bubbles, my breath short and ragged.

Trembling like I've escaped with my life, I am purified.

—

For our final day, they let us choose our own activity; without even thinking, we chose the beach. We wrap bottles of wine in our towels and hide them in our bags. We didn't bother putting on clothes and wait for the bus in our bathing suits. But even the excitement of the outing can't hide the exhaustion on our faces from the Olympic challenge we've just endured. Sunglasses hide our puffy eyes. No fattening meal has filled our emaciated bodies. Our muscles strain under thin, tanned skin pierced by our shoulder blades.

On the way, we pass the Pessac vineyard one last time. In the fields, the grapes have gorged themselves on sun, waiting to be picked.

They let us out at Arcachon. The Cap Ferret is ours for the day. We run top speed for the beach, throwing our towels in a sandy pile, letting the wine heat up in our bags. This is our last chance to swim in the ocean before we go home tomorrow.

The end of the summer has already cooled the water. I wade in cautiously, anciently, my skin shrivelled with a new kind of fatigue. My back peels in the low sun; I can roll off the ribbons of pink flesh.

Lace takes my hand and we dunk our wrists in the water up to our thighs, gazing into an endless horizon beyond which, somewhere, is Toronto. The sand gives way beneath our feet. All around us little fish swim, covered in grey foam. We let them nibble on us, smiling one smile. The sky hangs heavy with a coming storm.

The water ripples around us, calmly breathing, thick with suspended sand. I chew the wind as a weight settles into my stomach. A soft cramp. The heaviness is still inside me, swimming, growing, taking root.

We finally go under, still holding hands. Together, we swim a little distance, giddily matching the stroke of our free arms. We hook feet, creating a sea creature. We nearly choke, laughing at our absurd conjoined swim. We sink and float and crawl. The fish have gone, and the waves have picked up. We continue jerkily, a little more agile.

Lace lets go and rolls on top of me. I keep her on the surface as she moves us forward, her chest fitting together with mine. Against my belly, I can feel hers, the naked skin between our bikinis sliding, tickling. She covers my mouth with hers, licks my cheeks. I kiss around her nose. Our hair intertwines, and we wrap around each other in the same burst of laughter.

Beneath us, the depths have opened. The shore is impossibly far. Our microscopic friends are waving and calling from the beach, their forms howling.

The abyss below starts to drag me into its void, the bottom much too deep. We exchange a panicked look before launching into a crawl for our lives. The resistance is incredible. As we swim against the current, every stroke takes us farther away.

Baïnes.

I beat the surface with my arms and legs, getting nowhere, while Lace does the same beside me. The current rears up from the depths, pushing us out to sea. I whip the water, my crawl strong and sure. My muscles cramp, but I ignore the pain and keep pace. I breathe into a wave and choke, but keep going, my competitive instinct awakening. I kick twice as hard, my thighs burning, my shoulders forcing forward like I never thought possible.

To my left, Lace is a flat horizontal, going the wrong way despite swimming as hard as me. I hold my breath and go under, trying to trick the current deeper down. The silence engulfs me as I squint through the troubled water, blinded, doubting my direction. I change my kick to a fishtail flutter, switching up my resistance. When I lift my head the beach seems a little closer; I've made some progress. I search for Lace, but she must have dived too. I go back under, smoothing out my strokes to escape the current. My throat pulses with the need for breath and I surface again in the same spot. My eyes fill with blood from the pressure, and I'm lost, guessing at the shore. I flail on the surface, my movements frenzied. My arms and legs thrash independently. But I move. I swim desperately as a series of waves crash into me, and I gasp for air. How has the tide suddenly reversed? I dive under again, away from the sound of distant cries. I have to escape this water. My foe.

My leg cramps up. I can't go on.

Then suddenly I'm struggling, hitting the bottom and the surface together.

In one swift move, I'm flung onto a board. There's a motor, there are voices, there's a roar. I throw up from my mouth and nose, the pulse throbbing violently in my throat. Through my dizziness, I can't make out the jet ski or their shouts to know where Lace is. Clinging to the rescue board, I slap against the waves. We make a sharp turn and head out to sea. My cheek sticks to the plastic and I drool, spent, directionless, riding the surface of the lethal baïnes.

I peer down from a watery precipice as weeds sprout up like tentacles through my innards.

Part Four

❧ I ❧

FROM WHERE I SIT on the diving board, I rest my chin on my knees and cast my gaze wide across the pool. The main lights just went out, leaving only the emergency ones. The water's surface is still. Even in the dark, I can tell you every contour and imperfection, its topography imprinted on me.

We're not allowed to stay after hours, but he made an exception for me. He wants me to reacquaint myself with the space as part of my grieving process, but all I can see is Lace sleeping at the bottom. I wasn't watching as she got lost in the Atlantic and couldn't stop her from drifting away. But I brought her back with me. In the darkness, she's always there, her open eyes watching me for all time. She was there all through practice;

I finished my laps looking down at her. She saw my rounded belly and said nothing.

When you look up from the bottom, the pool appears natural, the waves lapping invitingly. Is that her down there like a playful imp holding her breath, stretched out against the polished concrete? The bubbles in her nostrils don't escape to the surface; they're pearls that stop her breath. She lies there unblinking as the chlorine eats her eye sockets.

I dive deep from my perch to join her, to kiss her blue lips.

One last look before I go. She doesn't react.

—

Vicky, Alexie, and the boys are all sitting together on the lounge sofa, waiting for me in a sleepy pile. Empty cans litter the ground, a fly buzzing in the mess. I fall into them and they engulf me, their affection warming me, suffocating me like a cushion. I snuggle in deeper.

I'm feverish with an autumn cold. My upper lip sweats, though it's not hot, and I shiver against my friends' bodies. When I open my eyes, I'm in my own bed. They've covered me in a clean sheet that I hold against my face, breathing in the sweet laundry smell. I teeter between sleeping and waking, wavering between two states, nauseous. My forehead throbs with a deep migraine, the pain supreme. My spittle stains my pillow.

The morning light informs me that practice is in less than an hour.

I pull on two sweaters, rummage in the pill bottles next to my bed, and throw a wet bathing suit in my bag. My bedroom smells sour, acrid like sickness. I'm in the pool before I know how I got there. The chlorine burns my nostrils, the water chills my neck, my bathing suit slices into my shoulders and legs. The discomfort is all-encompassing. A pressure in my chest keeps me from filling my lungs, and I drain myself trying. My head spins, and a cramp engulfs my calf. I try to ignore the pain, but every stroke seems to sink me.

I know perfectly well it's Lace, hanging relentlessly from my torso by her arms, her heavy embrace like an anchor. I struggle to the side, cough up a wad of phlegm, and tear off my goggles.

He grabs me by the arm and pulls me out of the pool like a toddler, his words vicious. I blow my nose in my hand and wipe it against my thigh, trying to look mad. But he doesn't care. He's not interested in my moods and takes my fever as an insult. I can't use Lace as an excuse anymore. He tells me that they're expecting me at the clinic on the weekend.

Then he dismisses me into the pool with a wave of his hand.

I shiver, resuming my sloppy swim, pushed by the wake of Alexie, who's tracking me in an attempt at motivation. When I finally finish my laps, I cling to the side like a life preserver, and pee a burning stream that warms my thighs. Alexie helps me out of the pool, holding me up as we walk to the team. I sit between her legs, my head heavy on her shoulder.

The World Cup will take us out west at the end of the month. To Edmonton. Or Calgary. I'm not sure I heard right. I struggle to stay awake next to Alexie. He wants us to focus on our relays and has reconfigured the teams to account for losing Lace. I'll be swimming second now. He announces that Steph will be our new starter and assures us she'll be ready. She beams at us. Vicky, Alexie, and I stare blankly back. We thought it went without saying that the event would be cancelled, but I guess he didn't see it that way.

The cloud of my fever overtakes me. I can't breathe in my bathing suit and burst into a coughing fit that enflames my throat. I suffocate trying to catch my breath. I feel Alexie's hand on my back as I'm blinded with tears. I spit and curse my way to the locker room, quaking with rage.

∾ 2 ∾

I GLANCE AT the familiar landmarks of the waiting room; the receptionist's face lit blue by her computer monitor, the strange painting of the calcified forest. The team isn't with me this time, but two old women in shawls sit up very straight in the worn armchairs. Their faces are a muted grey, like their hair, their lips lost in folds of skin. In their old age, they resemble each other, like sisters. But the distance between them and the fact they aren't talking suggests they're strangers.

I didn't bring anything for the wait, just a heavy scarf to muffle my shivering.

Wooly knots have formed in the hair at the base of my neck, and I try to untangle them with my fingers. I hook the roots and shake out the strands, never making it to the ends. When I pull, a ball of hair comes free, and I drop it at my feet. The tangles never end; the more I pull, the more I make.

The old ladies clutch their purses in their laps until one of them is called. She shuffles stiffly on the thick columns of her legs while the other watches me, coughing into an old tissue she then stuffs up her sleeve.

I can't hear anything from the exam rooms. This is a waste of time, but it's the team doctor, and if I leave before the consultation, they'll tell him. I slide down on my seat, stretching my legs out straight and an arm on either chair beside me like a starfish.

They finally call me and a pastel-clad nurse leads me down the hall. My sandals slide along behind her on the industrial carpet. She brings me to an exam room and starts by weighing me and taking my blood pressure. All my numbers are exactly the same, while absolutely everything is different. She leaves me sitting with my feet dangling at the edge of the bed. The paper sheet crinkles beneath me, ripping slightly. I poke my finger in the hole and rip it more.

When he walks in, I don't raise my head. I can smell him: a blend of musky, viscous cologne, hair gel, and strong deodorant. He opens my file, containing the standard forms detailing my near drowning and the death of my friend. With nothing to say, I press my lips together. He doesn't seem interested as he lays me back on the table; it's my insides he cares about. I tell him about the bleeding and how I'm sure it's been taken care of. He presses on my stomach, hovering at the edge of my pubic hair before pulling down my pants, smiling that I'm still not wearing underwear. He tells me what he's doing while he's doing it, inserting the words with his fingers. He's not wearing gloves and says he doesn't trust instruments. He works me manually.

The ceiling is made up of movable perforated polystyrene tiles. One of them has a thumbtack in it with nothing attached.

He's done.

The bleeding makes no sense, meaning everything is normal and the pregnancy is following its course. My saliva goes down hot. He gives me some flyers, telling me again that he wants what's best for me and will take care of the appointment to speed things up. It should be taken care of between now and next week. His words float around me in a haze, already evaporating.

He doesn't mention Lace. Or that it's her floating inside me.

———

I walk down Yonge with the wind in my face, wiping my nose in my scarf as the gusts bring tears to my eyes. I'm looking down at the filthy street when he appears suddenly, imposing, amid a meaningless crowd. The buzzard has taken his place in the margins. The homeless people sitting in the doorways don't see him. No one does. He picks up a scrap on the sidewalk, his naked neck bent over his prey, his heavy wings like a cloak across his back. His claws are retracted, having no grip on the concrete. I watch him devour his dinner, some kind of white meat he tears off in strips. When I try to pet him, he rears his head back indignantly and freezes, sizing me up. He wants no part of me today. I leave him to eat.

My own stomach twists with a furious new hunger, and I walk into the first pizza joint I pass. I devour my slice before I reach the door and consider ordering another one. In the door's reflection I see a trail of grease down my chin and wipe it off with my coat sleeve. I'm no less hungry. The pool is what I need. I turn at Wellesley to head back to the Athletic Centre, speeding up until I'm almost running. I want to dissolve, to immolate myself.

When I reach the turnstiles, my hair sticks to my forehead. Guido looks at me, horrified, and opens the access door without the usual routine. I chuck everything in my locker, the metal clanging accusatorily. I want to swim naked.

The water understands my state. I swim hysterically, calming my rage, expending my surfeit. I do lap after lap without coming up for air, beating out kilometres of rage. I sweat my bitter aggression into the chlorine. My muscles cramp, my intestines tear, I throw up pizza in the pool. The lifeguard on duty gives me a tired look, but I don't care. I just keep going, contaminating the pool with my base fluids, like I've done so many times before. Whether it's snot, piss, vomit, the water is always there, diluting me, digesting us like drowned corpses.

I stop when my body can't go on. My heart withstood the effort but takes off when I stand still. The lycra stretches against my convulsive heartbeat, and I breathe, sobbing, choking. I spit out a hunk of phlegm.

Against my thigh, I feel one of the jets. The filtered water is hotter than the rest of the pool, and the pressure makes a divot in my skin, seeking entry. I shift my leg, varying the tension. The force of the water caresses my buttocks, tracing the contours and curves. My lower back relaxes. I arch it, and the jet tickles my anus. With one finger, I pull aside the crotch of my bathing suit to let it inside. The opening contracts and my sphincter resists gently before spreading wide. The water pulses into me, my flesh vibrates, I bend over, ecstatic. The bubbles of my breath rise to the surface. I open my mouth and let the water play on my tongue. The pulse trembles between my buttocks, and I'm throttled by a ripple of pleasure. My body dissolves with the waves, the jet dispersing my orgasm.

I sit down in the drain, leaning on one hip to ease the pain. Up on his tower, the lifeguard sleeps with his face against his fist, the folds of his neck like a cowl. I float to the locker room in perfect calm.

∽ 3 ∾

AUTUMN HAS STRIPPED the carcass, leaving only white bones poking out from the tufts of dry lawn. The thorax forms a cage that extends from the jawbone, pointing upwards. It still has its teeth. All that's left of the tail is the long, bony column. I don't recognize it anymore and am afraid to touch it in case it falls apart. I linger a moment before leaving it there.

I slink back to my bedroom, drained. I'm supposed to be studying. My textbooks wait on my desk for decryption, unfinished notes accumulating in messy stacks. I steer clear of them. The floor is buried in dirty clothes and my still-packed suitcase sits in the corner. It's been months and I've only gone in for a few essentials. An infectious odour hangs over everything; I've stopped looking for its source.

On the other side of the wall, Lace's room sits untouched. We don't go in there anymore. Her parents still pay her rent but haven't come to pick up her things. Time has stopped in there. I sometimes hear her snoring at night, our beds only separated by a thin sheet of cracked plaster. She used to get under the covers with me after a disappointing night. But not anymore. Now, the nights hold only her absence.

I stare at the ceiling and imagine walking on its bare surface, stepping over the doorframes. A stark, upside-down world where the dull light fixture becomes a floor lamp. The mess stays at the bottom. But my spinning head brings me back to reality, to my room's accumulation, and reminds me there's no exit.

—

We get our copies back. I failed the exam. Alexie barely passed, but she's fine with that. We sigh and she lays her head on my shoulder. Her hair smells like coconut oil. She runs it through every night with her fingers, then ties it up in a colourful, grease-stained scarf.

I'd like to see the auditorium fill with water so the desks float, drowning the whole aquarium of us.

The class goes by and I don't catch a word. Alexie

is asleep against my shoulder when I realize it's over. When she wakes up, she's starving and we agree to Tim Hortons.

On College Street, the counter is packed with the obese and mentally ill from the CAMH next door. The addicts, like us, are easing their pain with sugar. Ahead of us in line, a man belches, already digesting the anticipated junk. His pants hang down past his underwear while his shredded jacket rides up his back. He smells rancid, buttery and aggressive. Alexie makes a loud comment and he turns to us with a toothless smile.

We place our order and the cashier raises an eyebrow. Alexie nearly drops our teeming tray. In record time we cover the table in crumpled paper, our bellies folding over the tops of our pants. We laugh, happily sated.

Alexie suggests some vintage shopping in Kensington, and we drag ourselves there. The stores are empty at this hour. Men stand smoking in front of their shops, in no hurry for customers. The smoke disappears in the awnings.

Alexie walks purposefully into a store to our left. I wander through the aisles. The smell of dead flesh, as strong as dried blood, seeps through all the secondhand items. Even after washing, they'll still have that withered smell. There are shelves full of costume jewellery, glasses, ties, and scarves. Alexie picks things up and puts them down, turning over tags. Bright, colourful fabrics lie heaped in joyful disarray up to the rafters. Alexie strokes a flannel shirt. When something catches her attention, she turns it inside out to check the seams and topstitching. I leave her to her appraisal, moving to a jumble of furniture and dusty dishes at the back of the store. I recognize the cut glass from when I was little, the same floral patterns. A coat rack like the one I found stands behind a pink velvet sofa holding a sign that says, "no seating." A gold tray full of chipped champagne flutes covers the surface of a low wicker table. There's a reading lamp with no shade, a rattan armchair with no seat, then behind a teak buffet I notice an old anatomy diagram. A human cross-section is shown from two different angles, the muscles defined with arrows. The glass is broken, but the wooden frame is intact. There's no price. I pull it delicately from the pile. It's mine.

∾ 4 ∾

I COLLAPSE IN a strange armchair, an empty beer dangling from my fingers. My ears ring. Vicky is dancing alone, barefoot, on a crumb-covered carpet. Seth is kissing a girl who might be Steph, but I'm not sure. Then I remember we're at his house. Someone passes me a joint and I take a few drags before pulling my hood down over my eyes. The ringing stops and I manage to stand.

The apartment is packed with people I barely know. I spot Mel behind the counter in the kitchen and drag myself over. His pupils are dilated and he can barely stand. I slide my hand into his and get another beer, leaning against his chest. Two guys I don't know are taking everything out of the fridge, trying to make an omelette. The pan clatters to the ground and they get down on all fours and lick it up, encouraged by the laughs around them. Seth gets annoyed and threatens to kick us all out. They calm him down by leading him to a platter striped with cocaine dregs. I finish my beer leaning on Mel, who's fallen asleep standing up. My stomach churns and I sit on the ground to cool off.

Seth's kitchen looks just like ours, with painted wood cupboards over plastic countertops and the floor finished in chipped, stained tiles.

The cramp is insistent. I curl into a ball, the cold floor soothing against my cheek. When I close my eyes, everything spins in the blackness. Mel comes over and snuggles in, like the small spoon. Legs overhead threaten to stomp us and Mel gets kicked in the knee, but doesn't respond. I have to get out of here. With my arms around his middle, I drag him down the hall to a bedroom and we fall into an unmade bed that might be Seth's. I put my hand down his pants and fall asleep holding his hard-on.

—

I have an appointment at the Bloor West clinic at Jane Station this afternoon. The team doctor set it up. Other than the prescribed pills, I've been forbidden to eat since yesterday. I wait for the elevator to the fourth floor with a woman and her grey-faced partner. The waiting room is filled with women of all ages. No one speaks. I fill out the forms without taking off my coat and wait around with my hands in my pockets. A woman dries her eyes with the tissue she just used to blow her nose.

I'm amazed to be called first. The glances cast toward me are filled with goodwill; we're all in the same boat.

The doctor speaks softly in clichés, unfazed by my indifference. She calmly explains the procedure, taking her time to detail the possible complications before handing me a pastel gown.

The nurse covers my belly in lubricant for the ultrasound and pokes the wand around my already rounded stomach. At twelve weeks, the embryo is visible. I turn my attention to the pile of clothes strewn on the chair, my inside-out sweatshirt, my pants on the ground.

They sit me up for the anaesthetic IV, and I watch the needle lift the vein in my hand. The liquid burns a little and my fingers go numb. With my hips at the table's edge and my feet in the plastic stirrups, they insert the speculum. My body jolts. It clicks inside, but I feel nothing. The suction noise only lasts a few minutes, but I have to tell them what I feel while it goes on. I feel like I'm shitting; I can't tell which hole they're working in.

It's over before I realize that Lace is gone. They extracted her into a bloody bottle I'm not allowed to see, her bones ground up into jam on its way to the waste chute.

The nurse strokes my forehead and leaves me to rest. I hiccup a long time on the canvas pillow, my cheek wet with snot.

❧ 5 ❧

THE TEAM TAKES up a whole gate at Departures, stretching out the shortened night piled on top of each other in our competition gear. Vicky sits between my legs with her head on my knees. I twirl her hair around my fingers and she purrs like a cat. Alexie sleeps on my shoulder, far enough from Steph so she knows we don't approve.

Pete and Seth are eating chips, getting crumbs everywhere. He's on the phone with Mel, furious that he's late and is going to make us miss our flight to Edmonton.

Behind the counter, the airline staff compare manicures. They have straight white teeth and bleached blond hair, like movie stars. Their nails click on invisible keys as they sneak looks at us, giggling about the boys and their muscles. Pete notices, wipes his chip-eating hand on his other sleeve and saunters to the kiosk. He drapes himself over the counter, talking with his eyebrows high, grinning like a little boy. They burst out laughing and he slays them both in one go.

I finish Alexie's smoothie as they announce flights that are never ours. Time wears on, so he repeats his instructions; we won't have time to stop at the hotel, we'll go straight from the airport to the club for the first events. We won't get time to warm up, so we'll do it on the bus and the flight, along with our focus drills. He snatches the chip bag from Seth's hand and holds it up to show us precisely what he doesn't want.

Mel runs in, face flushed, clutching a half-packed bag. The alarm didn't go off and the taxi was late. He yells at us all on Mel's behalf, pointing his finger at everyone. It's our fault. Mel endures it quietly. I pick up my coat to make room beside me just as they call our flight. We get to pre-board.

A few dozen bags are hefted in the chaos. Vicky herself brought three and asked to have them loaded as special items. The squeeze for time means we couldn't check them, and security took two tubes of moisturizer that exceeded the limit. Our shoulders bend with the weight. We show our IDs, Pete gets the number of one of the airline girls, and we finally board.

Steph is up first, already on the block; I'm behind her, then Alexie, then Vicky. The German girls have huge shoulders. One of the American girls dives too soon and we have to start over. When Steph takes off, I get in position, my heart already racing. I ignore a stomach cramp to execute a perfect crawl, earning precious millimetres for Alexie when I touch the side. My lungs still burn as I climb out and glance at him. I passed. Vicky finishes the relay with fierce concentration, and we come first. We're going straight to the finals. I don't swim again until the solo competition tomorrow, so I can breathe for a bit.

I sit next to Seth on the bleachers and he puts his arm around me proudly. My jammer cleaves my chest, but I'm too weak to take it off, so I just tolerate the pain. The youngest swimmers line up for the solo event; Steph has to swim without resting. The ballerina-haired judges assume their spots as the crowd cheers us on in their harsh, Western accents.

Seth notices the bleeding. The water has diluted it, and I'm sitting in a little pool that almost reaches him. He's not disgusted; he's worried. He takes my hand and delivers me to Alexie to deal with my girl business. She wraps her towel around my waist and directs me to the locker room. That's when he notices something's not right. He leaves the four hundred metre to come over, already exasperated. I can't hide from his questions and he's chased off Alexie, so I have no allies. He goes pale when I tell him, more worked up than ever, with one irrelevant question: Who? He won't accept that I don't know. There's just one right answer.

Behind him, the boys have qualified, but he pays no mind, insisting instead on shaking an answer from me that I don't have. I stare at his taloned feet in his plastic sandals. He turns his rage next to the team doctor, demanding to know why he wasn't informed, furious that he was left out. He promises me this doesn't end here. An official comes to find him, and he leaves for a moment, turning back first to let me know he's not done with me.

I'm hungry and his moods don't affect me anymore. I'm sick of his anger, sick of him, and dreaming of a salty poke bowl. I look for Alexie to escape this pool. I also have to deal with the blood.

Mel appears, shining and worried. I'm ready to go. That's all he needs to hear.

—

The restaurant is packed. The whole team came along. The tables are tiny, so we sit four to a bench, sending Steph to the bar with the kids; I don't want her with us.

Pete complains there's nowhere for him to put his legs, and whines that he's not allowed to drink. A burned smell works into our clothes. Something got ruined.

They don't have poke, so I order the crab cakes. The hot sauce stings my tongue. Vicky takes the bacon out of her salad and the boys roll their eyes. Mel checks his phone for the stats of the team we're up against tomorrow and we move in close to look at his screen. The Russians' times don't seem possible, but we all know they're pumped up on drugs. Last year, Seth got a retroactive gold medal after the Federation's inquest. It hangs over the toilet in his apartment with the word *fucker* written in Sharpie on the peeling wall beneath it. This year he's ready to beat their performance-enhanced asses in the first round, bragging about his progress, shouting defiantly at them in the restaurant they're not in. We have to calm him down when the server threatens to throw us out. We order more junk. My cramps seem to have passed. I should have gotten the steak, for the iron, but as of a few months ago meat grosses me out; it makes me think of the raccoon, maggots crawling on every plate. And Lace's corpse at the bottom of every pool. I leave the restaurant without paying.

The hotel is right across the street. I forget my room number and stand in the labyrinth of identical doors, searching for a landmark. When I turn the next corner, he's there. I freeze, ready to run, but I've lost control of my limbs. He fixes me predatorily through slitted eyes, grabs me by the armpit and throws me on the bed. I go to speak, but he stops me with his hand. I expect more interrogation, but it's about tomorrow's event.

The analgesic from the procedure could show up on the doping test. The team doctor knows the restrictions, but he's worried the clinic didn't follow procedure. He ordered the report and is waiting for them to fax it to him, when he's got much more important things to do. I'm not his only, nor even his biggest concern. Soon enough, I won't be anything. I might get penalized. Or cut from the team.

He kicks me out into the deserted hallway of closed doors.

∾ 6 ∾

MY ARMS SMACK the water so hard that my shoulders are airborne. I don't see the ceiling above me, just a perfect line ahead. When I'm almost at the edge, I instinctively calculate my distance and dive for a controlled turn. I didn't see the judge note my push-off—I'm already down at the other end. With my back in the water, knees out, I have a slight lead. The crowd noise hits me like stifled thunder, an animal roar, but it's not me they're cheering for; when my hand hits the side, I'm second. Another girl is already up on the starting block in goggles, cap snapped tight. Vicky helps me out of my suit so I can breathe. I cough, spit on the ground, and go join the team under our banner.

He doesn't congratulate me or even glance in my direction. His face is somehow bonier than before, his cheekbones poking through his thin, grey skin.

I pull on my training top and it sticks to me, I pull up my hood and my hair drips down my back. I gulp down half my water bottle. I've danced these steps so many times, I've had enough. I stare too long at the timer on the wall, hypnotized by the four hands ticking the seconds by. Lyle. Their movement calms me a little, but I can't grasp that I'm fainting.

I wake up flat on a bench with my feet on a pile of towels. No one's watching; we faint all the time. No one even notices anymore. One time, a guy was rushed to the hospital on a stretcher and the meet went on like nothing had happened. Speeding heart rate, nerve damage, asthma attack, dehydration, muscle sprains, dislocations, they don't even register. If you leave, you're replaced. If you're tired, they leave you behind.

I should be watching Vicky and Alexie in the two-hundred-metre backstroke, but I don't really care. I have a few hours to kill before the medal ceremony, so I make my way to the locker room and close myself in the bathroom stall. Though I don't need to go, I pee a clear stream through the fabric of my bathing suit.

—

When they hang the silver medal around my neck, I force a smile that cracks my face. The picture will be awful.

He stands out from the crowd, his pale eye like a hole in his face. I feel like I should apologize, though I don't know why.

The doping results came back negative, and I stand on the second step as the cameras flash. Behind them, Seth mimes popping a champagne bottle. The pool sleeps calmly after our abuse, the blue nuance of its neglected depths once again sovereign. We don't need the markers at the bottom; we all know our way. Someone hands me a bouquet of flowers, I don't know who. I sneeze in the petals, dying for a smoke.

Others step up to take my place on the podium. I'm not sure where to put the flowers. I stuffed the medal in the bottom of my bag with my water bottle and some used tissues, like we all do. Our return bags to Toronto carry gold, silver, and bronze, plus a new banner, which he took, folding it solemnly in triangles like the flag at a veteran's funeral. The equipment is stowed. We leave the pool.

———

The tower shoots up, disappearing past the grey skyscrapers. The UP Express bypasses the highway, blowing the dry yellow grass along the tracks. With just neglected back lots for scenery, Toronto holds out a miserable welcome. The city sprawls low and dim like the end of an overcast day. The houses with their narrow yards pass by indistinguishably, just a long row of brown brick. An ashen parade.

The robotic voice announces stations that aren't mine and the passengers converge blindly in the doorway. The car isn't crowded, but people stand anyway. Ahead of me, a woman coughs into her surgical mask, staring into the shapeless cityscape.

I get off at Dundas and walk to the streetcar, the strap of my bag cutting deeper in my shoulder with every step. The street is crowded, but lifeless. The houses lining the street look tired; sagging staircases beyond repair and low fences that protect from no one. In their windows, dirty drapes hide anonymous lives. The summer flowers have died and hang dry in the brush, strewn with garbage. On the sidewalk, I pass faded women and furrowed men of indeterminate age.

The same crowd rides the streetcar, same worn faces, spent by the same grind. Only children and the mentally ill bother speaking.

I walk up Kensington dragging my bag between the garbage cans where gloved women dig, the bins spilling onto the sidewalk. In front of a blue house, there are stacked boxes of dishes, clothes, books, a mattress ...

I pick through damp fabric and tarnished spoons. The covers of discarded books curl back, the boxes split. Tucked between two pages is a photo of a little girl in front of a low pine tree.

I pin the photo up over my bed. Still in my coat and sandals, I lie out on the bare sheet. The apartment is quiet. Alexie and Vicky decided to go out partying with the rest of them. Unable to go on, I dumped my bags just inside the door. I had planned to go right to bed, but sleep won't come. I listen for the source of whisperings I know are in my head. The top of the coat rack taunts me from beneath layers of dirty clothes. The base is hidden as well. Behind it, the anatomy diagram disappears in a sea of flotsam, textbooks, bags … there's clutter everywhere. The smell of rot permeates the room. It's the stench doing the whispering, punishing me.

I turn to the wall to escape.

My door slams against the wall and I jolt awake as Alexie bursts in. I slept for a whole day. They just got home and they're frantic. I can't believe the darkness outside belongs to the next day. Today became tomorrow and I didn't even notice. Alexie demands that I get out of bed, and pulls at my arm, but I push her away furiously. The door slams again, like a profanity.

❧ 7 ❧

THE SHEET CRINKLES with the dried sweat of the past days. All around the bed are dirty dishes, chocolate bar wrappers, crumbs, and crusts. I blow smoke out the window from a cigarette I smoked down to the filter watching the skeleton across the street at the edge of the porch. It looks like the ribcage has been crushed or has collapsed. I squint at it, but can't make it out. I light another cigarette off the butt.

I want to go look at the raccoon, but I'm deterred by the cold breeze outside. I'd need to put on a coat and maybe even a scarf, and I have no clue where they are.

Vicky and Alexie have stopped trying to draw me out. At practice, they say I have the flu, a stomachache, tendonitis, contradicting stories I'm sure no one believes.

166

The woman across the street comes out to smoke at her usual spot on the steps. When she's alone, she still sits in the same place, leaving her friend's seat empty. She's wearing a coat, open over what looks like pajamas. Her hair has grown, showing some brown roots. She looks exhausted. I inhale slowly with her in the silence of the apartment, and the smoke escapes in plumes through the open window, swirling away outside. My being revives with this exhalation. I toss the butt. Smoking made me hungry.

To leave my room, I have to walk in the piles of discarded clothes covering the floor. My fridge shelf is empty, so I steal two slices of bread and some butter from Alexie, a hunk of cheese from Vicky. I jam it all in without even making a sandwich, licking the butter off the knife to help it slide down. Mouth stuffed with cheesy paste, I dig through the empty rooms.

Alexie's room is bigger than mine. Her bed is made up, with a blue wool blanket folded at the end. Above her empty desk, her textbooks are arranged in order of size, with trophies on either end to hold them upright. The wooden dresser is filled with neatly folded clothes that smell like detergent. I touch the edge of a stack without disturbing it. She keeps her competition wear in the bottom drawer, bathing suits, training gear, goggles, towels, an uncovered box full of medals. Her underwear and sensible cotton bras are in the top drawer, nothing too fancy. In a cutlery divider, she has hair accessories: bright elastics, horn hairpins, different styles to go with her outfits. On her windowsill, Alexie grows plants. She's speared avocado seeds to soak in little glasses.

I pull back the velvet curtain that acts as Vicky's bedroom door. Having moved in once we were already here, she got the study alcove. I suppose she could ask for Lace's room now, but she hasn't. A clothesline stretches across the whole space, where she hangs her silks, chiffons, bathing suits. On her night table, a bedside lamp stays lit to make the place look brighter. Her window looks out onto a building that hides the sun even in summer.

I jump when I see her sitting on the bed. She doesn't seem upset about me violating her space. She pats the spot next to her and I fall into her arms. Her shirt smells like ladies' perfume and I drive my nose into it, shaking with sobs I can't hold any longer.

———

The notifications pile up on my home screen. I don't read a single word about missed appointments, questions, or threats. A squirrel runs across the telephone wire. I watch him until he disappears into the maple leaves. Where do squirrels die, if not in the road?

I need smokes. A pit deep in my stomach screams insistently with the tremor of light addiction. Head deep in the dirty pillow, I suck on a strand of my hair, waiting. Over my head, the little pine tree girl keeps watch.

I pull the edge of the photo and the tack rips through. The girl is small and blond, wearing a light-coloured dress buttoned up to her neck, high socks, and leather sandals. Her palms rest against her hips. She smiles with her mouth closed. She doesn't look like me. I slide the photo into the pocket of my coat.

Outside, it's getting dark. I think I'll go out.

It's colder than I expected and I'm not dressed properly. I flip up my collar, trying to remember the nearest convenience store. I should have gone right to Spadina, but now I have to go up Augusta. People speed up as the day ends and they filter from shop to shop, assembling dinner. I'd love nothing more than a complete, nourishing, colourful meal, prepared for me by someone else.

I point out my brand to the clerk. In the dark reflection of the store window, I see only the purple smudges under my eyes, darker in the shade of my hood. I light a cigarette so fast I nearly burn my hair with the lighter. I smile fizzily as the nicotine spreads through me.

I'm ready to go home, but when the doors of a streetcar open, I toss my newly lit cigarette and climb on before I know what I'm doing.

The warmth of the cramped bodies comforts me. They know where they're going, so I'll go there too. At every stop, I get pushed a little farther back, carried by the flow.

When the car empties out at Dundas Square, I step off with the rest of them and blend into the masses. A preacher is barking about the apocalypse through a worn megaphone. Two groups of shoppers pass each other at the intersection. In the centre of it all is a stage where a show is about to go on, lit by the giant video screen above. A hot dog vendor is surrounded by a hungry little crowd drawn to the smell of grilled onions.

I sit down on a concrete block and watch the technicians raise scaffolding, their calloused hands numb to the cold. They work without speaking, following some kind of plan. Passersby step over the electrical cords without noticing. A woman stops to answer her phone, her gold shopping bags strewn on the ground. The workers look at her and shake their heads.

A man sleeps on a heating grate, warm air blowing his sleeping bag like a friend.

In my pocket, I play with the edges of the photo, pulling my coat tight around me.

I find myself amid a bunch of loud boys and look up blankly. They hand me their joint. I take a few drags, burning my throat, and nod my thanks. A big bearded Black guy puts his arm around me, and I take a moment to enjoy the warmth of his winter coat before leaving him with a fist-bump.

The day has set on Yonge Street, already wearing the deep blue of winter night. The wind blows the hood off my head and my hair flies free. A few steps on, a sewer grate opens the sidewalk. The sound of the water underground calls to me with its familiar whisper. An invisible river taxis the used stream. I crouch down and hook my fingers in the grid. People walk around me, calling me names. I lean in until the metal meets my face, seeing only the shadows of the moving depths beneath. The edges of the concrete make a cylinder, a thick crust around the outer edge. My eyes adapt to the blackness, but the tributary keeps stealing away. In the sulfuric odour, I detect sediment and earth, hints of natural, unrefined waters. When I stand back up, the blackness of the street marks my face. I wipe my mouth with my sleeve. It smells like chlorine.

I throw my coat in a garbage bin with my sandals. The concrete is freezing.

I head down a narrow alley lined with dumpsters, broken glass crunching like sand beneath my feet.

© Helen Tansey

MARIE-HÉLÈNE LAROCHELLE used to be a competitive swimmer and is now an associate professor at York University. Her research and writing focus on invective, violence, and discomfort in literature, areas abundantly explored in her first novel, *Daniil and Vanya. Kiss the Undertow* (*Je suis le courant la vase*) was a French-language finalist for the 2022 Trillium Book Award. She lives in Toronto.

MICHELLE WINTERS is a writer, painter, and translator born and raised in Saint John, New Brunswick. Her debut novel, *I Am a Truck*, was shortlisted for the 2017 Scotiabank Giller Prize. Her work has been published in *This Magazine*, *Dragnet*, *Taddle Creek*, and the *Humber Literary Review*. She is the translator of *Daniil and Vanya* by Marie-Hélène Larochelle. She lives in Toronto.